IN SEARCH OF LOVE

After her mother's death, Laurel Smith learned the truth about the father she had never known. In a letter left for Laurel, her mother told her that her marriage to a man in America hadn't been good. When she had fallen pregnant with Laurel she had returned to England and written to tell her husband that she had lost the baby. Shocked, Laurel made up her mind to go and find her father, who had apparently been running a ranch in Colorado. But he wasn't the only man who was to change the whole pattern of Laurel's life . . .

SUZANNE CLARKE

IN SEARCH OF LOVE

Complete and Unabridged

LINFORD
Leicester

First published in Great Britain in 1996

First Linford Edition
published 2004

British Library CIP Data

Clarke, Suzanne
  In search of love.—Large print ed.—
Linford romance library
1. Love stories
2. Large type books
I. Title
823.9′14 [F]

ISBN 1–84395–159–2

Published by
F. A. Thorpe (Publishing)
Anstey, Leicestershire

Set by Words & Graphics Ltd.
Anstey, Leicestershire
Printed and bound in Great Britain by
T. J. International Ltd., Padstow, Cornwall

This book is printed on acid-free paper

1

'What's my name?' A hysterical giggle rose up into Laurel's throat at the man's question, but it wasn't aired, for at that precise moment she moved on her bar stool and the smooth linen of her dress slid beneath her, causing her to wobble slightly on the polished wood.

'Careful now!'

The stranger's arm immediately went around her slim waist to steady her. His green eyes, tiny crow's feet at their tanned corners, showed concern.

'How long did you say you'd been in Colorado?'

'I flew into Denver yesterday.' She looked up into the man's face. It was so familiar. 'And my name's Laurel Smith,' she added.

'Well, Laurel, didn't anyone warn you about altitude sickness?'

She shook her head.

'Initially, these high altitudes can have strange effects on your body. For example, your tolerance to alcohol is lessened. If I'd known you'd just got here, I'd have offered you a soda instead of another wine.' The kindly stranger, whom she guessed was in his fifties, left his hand on her. It was a gesture of protection, not of seduction, and she was grateful for it. 'Though I'm glad we met, Laurel.'

'So am I, Mr Richardson,' she replied honestly.

'Please, call me Jim.'

'OK,' she agreed, then over the country music playing on the restaurant's sound system, she heard the street door bang shut.

'What do you think you're doing in here?' a deep voice demanded behind them.

Feeling instantly guilty, she spun around. How could anyone know? Only her late mother's solicitor was party to the details of her trip. Jim's grip

2

tightened, and she was glad of it! A strikingly handsome man in his early thirties was standing barely two feet from her, his hands on the hips of his jeans.

'You know you shouldn't be here!' he chided. His gaze, as deep a blue as the freshly-laundered denim, was directed at Jim. A muscle ticked rhythmically beneath his firm jaw.

Laurel felt a little easier knowing the comment wasn't levelled at her, but not for long as that unfaltering stare suddenly turned on her. As the man took in the scene, noting the position of Jim's arm, he raised a dark brow in what she thought was surprise, or was it annoyance?

'One glass of beer with the guys isn't gonna kill me,' Jim replied amiably, then called out to the waitress to bring a bourbon on the rocks. 'I know my limit, Mac.'

I wish I did, Laurel mused, feeling most uncomfortable beneath the younger man's deliberate inspection.

His eyes, framed by thick black lashes, started at her head and slowly worked their way down her body taking in every little detail. The hairs on her arms and those on the back of her neck stood up as she shivered. The impact was like nothing she'd felt before. It frightened her.

Quickly reaching for her glass, she took a sip of the chilled Californian Chardonnay to moisten her parched mouth. She desperately wanted to run and hide. If it weren't for the alcohol, she may have packed up and driven away from the small town. But she couldn't; she was here for a purpose. Her fingers clenched the stem of the wine glass for fear it'd fall from her grasp on to the wooden floor.

The waitress set the stranger's drink on the bar between them. As the man leaned forward to get it, his bare, muscular arm momentarily brushed Laurel's. Its warmth seared her skin and immediately she recoiled as though she'd been singed by a branding iron.

Noticing her reaction, he gave a sardonic smile.

'You haven't introduced me to your friend, Jim,' he drawled, then sipped his drink, not taking his gaze from her face for a second.

'Laurel is visiting from England,' Jim explained.

'Is she?' came the indifferent reply.

'Yes, I am,' she interjected, irritated by being spoken of as if she wasn't there.

The man's penetrating stare hardened.

'For how long?' he enquired in a clipped tone.

'That all depends,' she answered defiantly, still annoyed by his attitude.

'On what?' The man pressed further, his long fingers closing tighter around his glass. Laurel's attention was drawn to the black hairs curling over the gold band of his wristwatch. They looked soft and silky in direct contrast to the overt hardness of his muscular frame and clear-cut lines of his profile.

5

'The area is beautiful and if everyone else is as friendly as Jim, I think I'll make this place the base for my holiday,' she countered.

Her earlier intoxicated sensation had gone and was replaced by obstinacy.

As the man took a sharp breath, his broad chest strained against the pale blue fabric of his shirt. Her pointed remark had hit a raw nerve though her sweet moment of victory was short-lived.

'You make a habit of picking up men in bars, ma'am?'

'I invited Laurel to join me,' Jim cut in as peacemaker, looking from one to the other. 'I was showing her some good old American hospitality. Hey, lighten up, Mac,' he added, punching the stranger playfully on the arm.

Draining his remaining bourbon in one gulp, the man slammed the empty glass down on the counter. The ice, which hadn't had time to melt, chinked loudly against the sides.

'I'll catch you later,' he told Jim,

deliberately ignoring Laurel but giving the other men at the bar a nod of acknowledgement before striding out into the street.

Laurel gave an inward sigh of relief, praying fervently she wouldn't meet up with that man again whilst in town.

'Mac's not always like that,' Jim explained, sensing her unease.

'I'm glad to hear it,' she replied, finishing her wine.

'Where are you staying, Laurel?'

'The Sunrise Motel,' she answered, picking up her handbag.

'I'll see you get back there safely.' Jim extracted some dollar notes from his wallet and threw them on the counter.

She went to get her purse from her bag but Jim's hand stopped her.

'I haven't paid for my meal, yet,' she told him.

'That'll more than cover it,' he said, refusing to accept her money.

'I can't let you pay,' she proclaimed.

'It's the least I can do. Mac's having a bad time. I don't want you getting the wrong impression of us,' he declared, standing aside to let her walk in front of him through the gangway between the tables.

Her muscles were tense when she reached the door. She was annoyed that Jim felt responsible for making amends for Mac's rudeness.

'You must let me repay you,' she insisted, not wanting him to think she was taking advantage of his kindly nature, too. 'Do you live in town?'

'No, on a ranch eight miles south of here. Do you like horses?'

'Yes,' she replied, feeling a blush come to her cheeks. With her mother, she rarely strayed from the truth as she'd always betray herself with a rush of blood to her face. Luckily, Jim didn't recognise the warning signs.

'Darn, it's a pity I can't help you out just now,' he told her. 'We run a great ranch but all our cabins are full at present.'

'I've heard it's expensive to stay on a ranch,' Laurel returned, pleased they were full. She loved most animals but horses did scare her. 'I don't think my spending money would stretch that far. I have enough to last for six months, so long as I'm careful.'

'Doesn't it worry you to travel alone?' he asked as they began to walk slowly up the street.

'Most of my friends couldn't afford the trip and those who could wouldn't be able to take six months leave from their jobs.'

'If you're happy in your own company, then it's fine.'

'I'm glad we got chatting, Jim. I hate to admit it but I was feeling a bit self-conscious when I was eating on my own. But I'm sure I'll get used to it.'

'Maybe we could meet tomorrow,' she suggested.

She turned to see him shake his head.

'We've got a large group arriving at lunch-time. We'll be busy for the next fortnight.'

'Oh.' She sighed despondently as

9

they strolled side by side.

The sun was now partly obliterated by the snow-capped peaks. The area was different from what she'd been expecting: though there were the Rockies' craggy mountains to the west and east, the valley itself was fertile and for early June, the evening temperature was very warm.

'I don't like being in your debt,' she persisted. Like a terrier refusing to let go of a rat's neck, she hung on to her principles.

Jim stopped suddenly and stared at her with a ponderous expression.

'What are you doing tomorrow morning?'

'I hadn't planned anything,' she said truthfully, shrugging her shoulders.

'Would you come out to the ranch for a couple of hours? I could do with some help. That's if you don't mind, Laurel.'

Her green eyes widened in alarm.

'I know very little about horses, Jim.' They had four legs, a mane, a tail and had thrown her on the two occasions she'd tried to ride one of them.

He chuckled deeply and began to walk to the motel's entrance.

'That's OK — our cook quit today so I need someone to work with me on the buffet lunch. We should have a replacement by tomorrow night.'

'That would be great,' she replied, stopping by her door. 'I love cooking.'

'I don't like cutting into your vacation time,' he confessed after giving her directions to his ranch.

She held her hand out to him.

'I'm already looking forward to seeing a real ranch,' she declared as he shook her hand and they said good-night.

After locking her motel room door, she flopped down on her bed and threw off her sandals. Closing her eyes, she immediately recalled her late mother. An invisible hand gripped her stomach and twisted it; the loss of her mother following her long illness was still painful.

She didn't have any close family with

whom to share her grief so her neighbours had rallied around and tried to console her. Although Laurel had been aware there'd be no remission, just deterioration, the end had nevertheless come as a huge shock. Only now, twelve weeks later, was she piecing together her own life, having constantly been at her mother's side for her final months.

Maybe Mr Saunders had been right, Laurel thought as the tears trickled down her face.

'Laurel, the past year has been traumatic for you,' she could hear the solicitor's voice saying just a week ago. 'You should think carefully before you do anything. You need time to adjust.'

But she hadn't taken his advice. She'd booked her flight with the local travel agent immediately after leaving his office. It was something she had to do. During her twenty-four years she'd been cautious, a trait which her mother had instilled in her, and for the first time, she'd done something on the spur of the moment. But was it now going to backfire?

* * *

Next morning, Laurel's jet lag ensured she was awake before the birds, though she didn't dare try to get back to sleep in case she'd be late arriving at Jim's ranch.

With heavy eyes, she avidly read the literature on the area which she'd picked up in the motel's reception when she'd checked in. Her mind kept straying to the dark stranger, Mac, whose presence had unsettled her in the bar and who later had infiltrated her dreams.

Why was she even thinking about him? She certainly wasn't interested in that type of man. When she settled she wanted it to be with someone who was gentle and treated her with courtesy. But that was all in the future, she thought, turning over a page, yet her brain wasn't fully concentrating on the text.

Remembering the way the stranger's eyes, like flashes from an uncut sapphire, had impertinently appraised her body made goose pimples erupt on her arms, even now.

As if he'd be interested in her anyway — she wasn't in his league, quite a shy girl whose figure was top heavy for her slim hips. How she wished she could be a stock size like her friends. They didn't have the hassle of finding a dress in a shop which actually fitted properly, a rarity for Laurel who'd taken to designing and making her own, out of sheer desperation.

Although Mac had been wearing what she considered typical ranch clothing, jeans and boots like Jim's, the stylish cut of his slightly curly black hair and the expensive watch made her believe he'd be more at home in a designer suit. Forget him, an inner voice warned her.

Don't worry, I will, she replied to it

silently. If she was lucky she wouldn't see this Mac man again. She would throw herself into helping Jim — and who knew where it would lead?

Going through her own creations several hours later, she decided to play safe and wear her new pair of jeans, topped with a white cotton, short-sleeved blouse. Although she'd be dealing with salad vegetables in the kitchen not livestock in the corral, she'd nonetheless look the part!

On her arrival at the ranch, which she reached by a dusty track from the main highway, she was met by Jim. He'd been sitting in the shade of the covered porch that ran the length of the white wooden, single-storey building.

'You're early,' he said as he opened the driver's door and helped her to her feet.

'Jet lag,' Laurel murmured, gazing around her in amazement. Set in the lush valley between the ranges of mountains, the pasture spread as far as she could see. Across the dusty track from her was a fenced corral.

Her muscles tensed immediately as she noticed horses grazing there. On the far side, some young men were sharing a joke by the stable block, and catching sight of Jim, they waved then disappeared inside.

'It's a killer,' Jim agreed. 'Though you'll find it worse when you head for home. It took my system four days to adjust when I went to London.'

'You've been to England?' she enquired, strolling with him to the building's main entrance.

'Many years ago,' he replied, with a dreamy quality to his voice. 'That's why I enjoy chatting to any English visitors who pass through. I really loved the time I spent there. It's why when I heard your accent I invited you to have a drink.'

'It was nice to see a friendly face.' Laurel smiled. 'And I enjoyed our chat. Haven't you ever wanted to go back to England?' she ventured further, walking up the wooden steps to the verandah.

'No!' His tone was suddenly stern. 'Nothing there for me now.' He turned to her. 'You don't want to hear my troubles, Laurel. The kitchen is this way.'

Following him through a Western-style lounge area and down a narrow hallway, she wondered what had made him react like that. She couldn't press the point as Jim obviously didn't want to talk about it. Maybe he'd open up later, she mused as he held open the door to the kitchen for her.

'This is it,' he remarked with a sweep of his arm.

The large room, white tiles covering the building's wooden walls, was fully equipped with gleaming ovens and freezers. In the centre was a scrubbed mahogany table which she felt wouldn't look out of place in an antique shop.

Seeing the direction of her inquisitive stare, he strolled over to it and stroked the wood lovingly.

'I've been around here for almost as long as this piece,' he told her, smiling.

17

'Your accent isn't the same as the other people in this area.'

'The reason for that is, I was born and brought up in Connecticut on the East Coast. I'm a Hartford man — a Yankee through and through, so my friends tell me.'

His imparted information shocked her, although it shouldn't have done.

'What is it that you want me to do?' she asked hastily, deliberately turning her stare from Jim to gaze at the vegetables piled on the worktop.

The cold meats were already prepared and only had to be laid out on platters. The salad vegetables took her the most time. As they worked, Jim cooking rice and pasta for the salads, they chatted easily about many things.

Jim didn't mention his background any more, nor did he pry into hers for which she was thankful. There were skeletons in her cupboard which couldn't yet be released. She had to be sure it was safe first to let them out and that could take a little while.

'You're a good worker, Laurel. How would you like a job here on the ranch?' he suddenly asked her when they were clearing up. 'For the next month or so.'

'I wish I could but I don't have a work permit. I wouldn't want to get in trouble with the authorities,' she answered despondently.

Blast! It was the ideal opportunity to be here, as Jim had instigated it, not her, and she'd let it go. Her heart twisted in anguish.

Jim leaned against the wooden table with his arms folded across his chest.

'That's a shame. Though if we were to provide you with board and lodging in exchange for you doing a few chores around the place, I can't see it'd cause a problem. You could pay us a nominal sum for your rent. It'd be cheaper than staying in a motel and you'd be able to get some riding lessons in, too.'

'That'd be great!' Laurel agreed, mustering up all the enthusiasm she could. Horses! That aside, she wanted to throw her arms around Jim and hug him but instead she wiped her fringe away from her moist brow. It was getting hot outside and with the burners of the gas hob all being used for Jim's dishes, her clothes were sticking to her.

'You've been a fantastic help to me,' he told her, taking note of her now dishevelled appearance. 'Why don't you stay for lunch and think it over?'

'OK,' she consented, although she knew there was nothing to consider. Her mind was already made up. It wouldn't be easy but it would give her thinking time to plan the best way to proceed.

'It's too late now to go and pick up your things from the motel,' Jim declared, startling her from her reverie. 'If you want to freshen up before eating, you're welcome to use the shower in my room.'

'That sounds wonderful,' she declared, wishing she had a cool dress or shorts with her to change into. Never mind, she'd feel refreshed after standing under the cool water.

'I have to go out for a short while on business. If I'm not back, wait for me on the porch,' he told her. 'And please, help yourself to a drink from the refrigerator.'

Then, following his directions, Laurel found his room along the hallway. In minutes, having peeled off her clothes, laying them carefully on his bed, she was standing under the fierce stream of water in his en-suite shower.

Closing her eyes, she let it pour over her hair and smiled secretly. She couldn't have engineered it better herself if she'd tried! Luck was truly on her side. Who knows — she may even get to like horses with tuition.

All of a sudden, she heard the bathroom door being thrown open. Grabbing a small towel she screamed and peered round the curtain.

'What on earth are you doing here?' a familiar deep voice demanded angrily.

'I could ask you the same thing!' she

21

cried, her heart thumping wildly from the shock.

The small towel she held was barely big enough to cover anything and Laurel was embarrassingly aware of this.

'I live here,' Mac replied, raising a mocking brow at her display of comic animation. 'What's your excuse, Laurel?'

'What does it look like?' she retorted, goose pimples erupting over her dripping body as Mac had now turned off the shower. 'Do you think I could have some privacy?'

'You haven't answered my question of what you're doing in Jim's room.' His deep blue eyes were regarding her stealthily.

Grabbing the shower curtain for extra protection, Laurel scraped her fringe from her face.

'Jim said I could use his shower because I needed to cool down.' Her heart was still hammering away in her chest.

'Really?' The dark brow lifted a fraction higher. 'I won't ask what you've been up to while I've been busy in the stables.'

As much as she wanted to argue the point with him, Laurel felt extremely vulnerable. Swallowing back the retort that none of it was his business, she muttered through gritted teeth, 'Would you please pass me a bigger towel?'

The tall man in jeans stood his ground. She didn't want to grovel to him and she certainly didn't have the self-assurance to step out of the cubicle while he watched her.

'You do realise Jim's blood pressure will be soaring sky-high,' he drawled, still not making a move.

Laurel was now feeling incredibly self-conscious.

His beaming smile, that lit up his features, surprised her. His even teeth were bright in contrast to his deep tan.

'And who could blame him?' he added, an evil twinkle coming to his eyes.

Taking the larger towel he was finally proffering, Laurel stared angrily at him.

'Does Jim know his ranch hands walk into his room uninvited?' she countered bravely while having to contend with the problem of holding the towel and the shower curtain to shield herself from his unfaltering gaze.

'Is that what you think I am?' He laughed gruffly.

'You've just said you've been working in the stables,' she replied, a lot happier when the towel was secured around her.

Grudgingly, she took his hand as he helped her out of the cubicle. It was rough to her touch but it was so very warm. Feeling as if her body had received a jolt of electricity from a summer storm, the tiny hairs on her arms stood on end. Water was dripping from her on to the tiled floor though Mac didn't move to leave. His closeness was unnerving her.

'Someone has to take charge,' he said, staring down at her.

His stature made her aware he'd be

good at that; ordering people around would come naturally to him. Like the previous evening, he was dressed in jeans, not the fashionable type available in boutiques but working ones, which emphasised his powerful thighs. A white T-shirt, tucked in beneath the black leather and silver belt, clung to his broad chest.

'Jim shouldn't be doing anything strenuous,' he went on sternly. 'But either foolishly he hasn't told you or you've deliberately chosen to ignore the warning.'

'What do you mean?' she cried in alarm, her hand clenching to a fist at her side.

'Don't play the innocent, Laurel. I saw the way you were acting last night and then I find you in his room to cool down.' He spat out the last words, his lip curling with distaste.

'How dare you assume . . . '

'No, I'm just a regular red-blooded male,' he retorted. 'As is my partner,' he continued. 'If it's willingly offered,

Jim'd be a fool to knock it back.'

'Your partner?' she echoed breathlessly. He had to be lying!

'We weren't formally introduced last night. Jim must have had other things on his mind.' His smile turned into a grimace. 'And we both know what that was.'

'So you are?' she prompted, ignoring his disparaging remarks.

'Brandon McGuire,' he informed her. 'Most people call me Mac. I'm the major shareholder of this ranch.'

She gasped in surprise. The way Jim had spoken, she'd believed he was running the place. If she worked here, she'd be answerable to this obnoxious man and not to Jim. It didn't seem such a pleasant scheme after all. And she thought luck was on her side!

'Would you mind if I got changed alone, Mr McGuire? Jim is expecting me for lunch and I wouldn't want to be late.'

The blue stare narrowed dangerously. 'I don't want you jeopardising his health, lady,' he said, emphasising his words by stabbing her chest bone with his index finger. 'Because if you do, you'll have me to answer to, and you should know I'm not a man to cross!' With that, Mac left as quickly as he'd arrived.

Like the previous evening, Laurel was left reeling. Her body was quaking all over. Nobody had ever affected her like this and she was frightened, realising his had been no idle threat. And what did he mean about Jim's illness?

Unravelling the towel, she began to dry herself slowly, her mind pondering on their conversation.

Why had she sounded so enthusiastic about the temporary job which Jim had offered her? She didn't want to turn it down, yet could she possibly work with that man hanging around, watching her every move?

A small voice in her head reminded her why she was here. For the rest of her life she might regret not staying on for at least a week. It would take a lot of courage, she knew. If Mac became insufferable she could easily leave — it wasn't as if she had a legally binding contract.

Pulling on her jeans, Laurel pursed her lips thoughtfully. As Jim's illness worried Mac, she doubted he would dare to upset her in front of his partner.

It was then she decided to stay on. Mac wouldn't get the better of her!

Her brave feelings soon melted away when she walked on to the veranda and immediately came face to face with Mac. He was talking with two men who'd recently arrived and were still in their casual travelling clothes. Noticing the warning look that was shot in her direction, she strolled over to Jim, feeling conscious of his stare every step of the way.

'Thank you for letting me use your room,' she said quietly, positive that even from this distance Mac would hear each word.

'It was the least I could do, Laurel,'

Jim replied, cupping her elbow and squeezing it.

Glancing across, she knew the action had been duly noted by his partner who was now heading towards them through the gathering.

'We meet once again, ma'am,' Mac drawled, acknowledging her with a dip of his dark head.

'Laurel's done a lot for me this morning,' Jim informed him, passing her a glass of chilled orange juice.

'Really?' Those eyes held a sardonic hint which she didn't fail to miss. But she pretended his comment was of no interest to her.

'I can see she's going to be an asset here,' Jim continued. 'We're missing the female touch around the place, Mac.'

Laurel nearly choked on her drink seeing Mac's expression.

'Have I missed something here?' Mac demanded, his temper barely under control.

'I've asked Laurel to stay and help us,' Jim explained.

29

'She doesn't have a work permit!' Mac hissed, lowering the volume of his voice, although his ire wasn't lessened. 'There's absolutely no way!'

'I'm not going back on my word,' Jim persisted. 'Laurel can stay in the main house as our guest. We have spare rooms.'

'This isn't the time or the place to talk,' Mac retaliated, glaring at Laurel. 'We'll discuss this at a more sensible hour. But I'll tell you right now I'm not happy with this situation.'

Jim shuffled uneasily when Mac had gone.

'I don't want to cause trouble,' Laurel insisted, wishing she had the inner strength to confront Mac. If he knew the truth maybe he'd be more understanding. One glance in his direction, she realised it would make things a lot worse — and she'd never get the opportunity to spend the night under the same roof as her father!

2

Shaking his head in disbelief, Jim replied, 'I can't understand what's got into him. For the last five years, Mac's never contradicted my decision when hiring staff. It's not as if you'd be permanent, Laurel.'

'As Mac said, it's probably not a good idea. I don't have a permit,' she replied sadly looking up at the man whose image was imprinted indelibly on her mind. Although his dark brown hair was now peppered with grey, he was still handsome and she could understand why her mother had fallen for him.

'If you were a friend of my family coming here for a vacation, you might want to help out, true?' His green eyes, the same hue as her own, twinkled.

'I suppose so.'

'Then that's what we'll tell everyone.

I used to know people in England so it isn't an outright lie.'

'You have family there?' she asked, nervously sipping her orange.

His kindly features hardened.

'Sorry, I didn't mean to pry,' she added hastily. She didn't want to spoil things now.

'It's OK,' he shrugged. 'It was a long time ago. My wife was English. When I saw you yesterday evening in the bar, you reminded me of her. Angie must've been about your age when we first met.'

There was no mistake, Jim was her father, yet it sounded peculiar to hear her mother called by the shortened version of her name. No-one had been allowed to call her Angie; she'd been most insistent on that. It was always Angela. Had it brought back so many memories — ones her mother wanted to remain buried?

'Do you mind me asking what happened?' she ventured, preparing to be told to mind her own business. Only last week she'd learned her mother's version of events from the letter, left with the solicitor for Laurel to read three months after her death. For all these years, her mother had lied to them both.

'We grew apart. You know how it is. Mac's grandparents were here at the ranch then. They tried to talk some sense into me but I was stubborn and refused to go after Angie.' His eyes turned on her. 'We all make mistakes, Laurel. There are some you can't undo.'

'So you've known the McGuires for years,' she mused aloud as she accompanied him inside the building.

'I remember when young Brandon was knee-high to a grasshopper,' he remarked, mimicking an Old Timer's voice.

She was chuckling when they entered the dining-room, unable to visualise young Brandon as anything but the strong-looking man who was currently mixing with the guests.

At one end of the room, the dishes she'd helped to prepare were set out on

33

a heavy-duty wooden table. Deliberately she held back until the guests had served themselves then she moved forward to get a plate.

Before her hand reached the top plate in the stack, another one got there first and held it out to her. Glancing over her shoulder, she murmured her thanks to Mac, who was standing just too close to her for comfort.

'You must be hungry after your exertion,' he said quietly, his warm breath against her neck making her shiver. 'You'd better take what you can, lady, because you won't be here for dinner!'

Refusing to rise to the bait, she ladled a spoonful of pasta salad then continued along until her plate was full, all the while conscious of Mac's presence a step behind her.

The guests were seated at a long table and the way they were sharing jokes, it seemed they'd booked the holiday as a group. From the several empty places remaining, Laurel chose one at the far end rather than be in the middle of them. Starting to eat, she was glad Mac couldn't annoy her.

But once again, he marred her attempt for peace and quiet. He pulled up a chair, setting down his plate so he faced the head of the table where Jim was deep in conversation with the man who appeared to be the group's leader.

'What have you got planned for us this year, Mac?' one man asked him.

'There's no way I'm going white-water rafting again!' an attractive brunette across the table from Laurel cut in. The woman's blue eyes flitted in Mac's direction, remaining there as she appraised him.

Forcing her attention back to her meal, Laurel decided the woman was welcome to him. Maybe it'd keep Mac occupied so he had less time to irritate her.

'The programme will be much the same,' he answered the man. 'If you don't want to go rafting, Chantelle, I'll arrange something more to your taste.'

Laurel cringed hearing his sensual drawl and all that it implied. Small wonder he thought the worst of her friendship with Jim when Mac's own morals seemed akin to those of a stud stallion.

'How are your plans going for the rebuilding of Passion?' another man interjected, pushing his empty plate aside and sipping his glass of beer.

'I've had setbacks this winter,' Mac replied, putting down his fork and beckoning to a young man who was bringing drinks to the table.

'I'll have iced tea, Billy,' he told the lad then turned the full force of his stare on Laurel. 'Ma'am?'

Bristling at the formal mode with which he'd purposely addressed her, she kept annoyance from her tone, replying levelly, 'Orange juice, please.'

Already Mac's attention had reverted to the former topic.

'There were heavy snowfalls and two buildings are now in danger of collapsing.'

'What a pity!' Chantelle proclaimed. 'It's so heavenly. I was looking forward to staying there next year. Can you imagine having a vacation in a place called Passion?' She giggled and looked pointedly towards Mac.

'Are you here for the riding?' the man beside Laurel suddenly asked, surprising her.

She glanced around at the man, whom she guessed was in his late thirties.

Carefully wording her answer, feeling the weight of Mac's stare upon her, she replied, 'Not especially. Colorado seems to offer a lot of opportunities for holidaymakers.'

Immediately the man — Gary, he informed her — seized on her English accent and they spent the rest of the meal chatting easily. Initially she'd felt Chantelle's critical gaze but the woman had obviously considered Laurel wasn't a threat to her potential — or was it a continuing — relationship with the now taciturn Mr McGuire.

'Laurel and I have a few things to sort out,' Mac declared when coffee was being served, the scrape of his chair on the wooden floor emphasising his impatience.

'I've enjoyed our chat,' Gary told her as she reluctantly got up from her seat. 'Perhaps we can have a drink tonight?' he ventured.

'Laurel.' Mac's tone sounded like a warning.

'I'll try,' she replied, irritated by Mac's interference and also by his firm hand that was gripping her right arm.

Not wanting to make a fuss, she let Mac guide her outside. To the guests it appeared Mac's arm was around her shoulders in a gesture of friendship, whereas she knew that he was frog-marching her away for another confrontation.

With any other man it might have felt comforting to have a strong arm propelling her into the protective warmth of his chest, but with Mac it was disquieting. Inwardly she began to shake but she fought to retain her composure. Nothing was going to stop her being with her natural father.

Stopping by the fenced corral, Mac spun her around to face him, letting go of her as if she had a contagious disease. His nose wrinkled in distaste.

'Just what game are you playing, lady?' he demanded furiously.

'I'm not playing anything,' she protested, her green eyes wide from shock at his vehemence.

'Maybe playing isn't the right word,' he spat out, his top lip curling. 'Perhaps I should say working at!'

'What are you insinuating?' Laurel cried, stepping away from him, though the white fence caught her in the back, preventing her from escaping.

Mac took a pace forward so he was barely six inches from her.

'Isn't it obvious?' he countered, his blue stare burning deep into hers. 'Two men in one day?' He tutted loudly.

'I'm not after anyone,' she insisted. 'I came here because Jim wanted — '

'I know, you've already told me — your help,' he interrupted sarcastically. 'So are you going to help Gary, too?'

'You won't listen to me!' she sobbed, side-stepping but he followed her action so he was even closer to her trembling body now. 'I wanted to help Jim because he wouldn't let me pay for my meal last night.'

A black brow twisted wryly but she hurried on.

'When he walked me to my motel, he asked if I'd come to the ranch today and I agreed.'

'I'm sure you did,' he returned icily. 'Jim may consider we need the feminine touch around here but I can see it ending in disaster. We don't need your services, lady.'

'We spent two hours in the kitchen.' Laurel sighed, her composure fading rapidly.

'Didn't it bother you that someone could walk in at any moment?'

Suddenly something brushed the top

of her head. In fright, she leaped forward, Mac's arms catching hold of her.

'What the — ?' Laurel cried in alarm, turning her head to find one of the horses by the fence.

Mac's deep laugh echoed in his chest which she was propelled against.

'Assunna won't hurt you, will you, old girl?'

'That's an unusual name,' she remarked, swallowing deeply and wishing Mac would let go of her. It wasn't just the nearness of the horse that was making her tremble.

'It means pretty lady in the Navajo language. She's worried she's got competition for my affections.' His hand stroked the mare's grey muzzle fondly.

'Then you can assure her that she hasn't!' Laurel snapped, trying to ease herself out of Mac's grasp. His arm was still holding her tightly. 'Not with me anyway,' she added, remembering Chantelle.

'No. You have your sights firmly set elsewhere,' he remarked, his fingers now raising her chin so she had to confront his enigmatic stare. 'If we were alone, we could accomplish a lot in two hours, Laurel. I guarantee it.'

His smoky, sensual drawl mesmerised her, though his words provoked a chill to travel down over her spine.

'As Jim and I did,' she said breathlessly, unable to tear her attention from his full lips which were dangerously close to hers. 'You've just eaten the fruits of our labours for lunch,' she added, swallowing away the dryness on her tongue. 'Jim couldn't get the work done alone before your guests arrived and he didn't have the time to find a replacement cook.'

'Then why didn't you explain what you were doing?'

'Because you didn't give me the opportunity!' she protested. 'As there only ever seems to be one thing on your mind, you assume it's all anyone else thinks about, too! Some of us just want friendships.'

'With older men,' he noted sarcastically. 'And preferably those with a healthy bank account.'

'Money is not my motivation, Mister McGuire,' Laurel replied, taking the opportunity to step back from him when his arms dropped from her. She felt oddly cold without their warmth, even though it hadn't been comforting to her.

'Really? Then your friendship with Jim will be put to the test if you're considering working here for nothing.'

'I've given him my word that I'll stay on for the next four weeks.' She held her chin up proudly.

'You won't last four days let alone four weeks!' he retorted, pointing to Assunna who was grazing on a clump of long grass by the fence. 'You certainly know nothing about horses.'

'She just surprised me. Besides, I'm a very fast learner,' she replied with renewed stubbornness — a trait she'd obviously inherited from her father. 'Jim's already agreed that I'll be doing a few chores around the house and not out here.'

'You'll go where you're ordered,' he declared and she cringed from the force of his words. 'You could, of course, tell Jim you've changed your mind.'

'And give you the satisfaction of seeing me off the property?' she parried.

'It'll happen sooner or later, so why not go now, Laurel, before you make a complete fool of yourself?'

Laurel was itching to wipe that smirk from his face. Why did she let him goad her? Her fingers curled into her palms, forming fists at her side.

She took a deep breath. Calm down, he isn't worth it!

'Because when I promise to do something, I see it through to the end, to the best of my ability, Mr McGuire,' she retaliated, giving Mac a sickly-sweet smile.

'We'll see,' he said, chuckling. 'You've

heard the expression — pride comes before a fall?'

'Yes,' she snapped, wishing she hadn't sounded quite so boastful about her capabilities.

'Well, I'll be waiting, lady, for you to fall on that pretty, little face of yours.'

Jim arrived suddenly, startling Laurel, whereas Mac just took it in his stride.

'Have you two come to an understanding or do you want me to act as mediator?' he asked, looking from her flushed expression to Mac's amused one.

'Oh, Laurel and I understand one another perfectly,' Mac replied smoothly, his raised brow warning her not to contradict him. 'Though don't you agree it'll be better if the guests consider Laurel a friend of mine? It'll explain why she's in the main house and not in the quarters with the other ranch hands.'

'I don't mind staying there with the other hands,' she insisted. Anything to get away from Mac.

From Mac's husky laugh, she knew she'd said the wrong thing — yet again!

'You'd enjoy sharing with eight men?' he queried.

'Mac, you'll drive Laurel away with this nonsense,' Jim cut in.

'Oh, he won't do that,' she said, smiling at her father. 'I know Mac's joking with me. This next month should be a lot of fun.'

'It certainly will,' Mac agreed, and from his smile she guessed it would be at her expense! 'So, Jim, what should we say if anyone gets too inquisitive? After all, you're the one who hired her.'

'I do have a name, Mister McGuire,' she retaliated pointedly, amazed at her new-found courage since meeting up with Mac.

'If you have a surname, ma'am, then you haven't informed us of it,' Mac responded, holding her blazing emerald stare.

'Smith,' Laurel confessed quietly.

'Can't you come up with something

more original?' he quipped in disbelief.

'Whether you choose to believe it or not, is up to you but it's the truth,' she said, wondering if Jim would realise her name was the same as his wife's maiden name.

'Then Miss Smith, I presume it's Miss not Mrs,' Mac said, glancing down at her left hand for the sign of a ring, 'if you're moving in today, I'd better show you to your room.'

Jim was regarding them closely and shook his head.

'I think we'll be safer if we say Laurel's a friend of the family. I was related to a Smith in England.' A dark cloud passed over his expression and for a few moments he was lost in thought. Remembering where he was, he patted Laurel on the shoulder. 'Mac will see to you — I have chores to attend to. I'll expect you for dinner this evening.'

Watching him amble off to the stables, Laurel wondered if she had made the right decision coming here.

She desperately wanted to get to know her father better, but had she brought him a heap of problems? Especially if Mac was right and he was ill.

'Are you coming?' Mac chided, interrupting her train of thought. 'I have guests who are hoping to begin riding today, not some time next week.'

Letting Mac lead, she kept at a distance behind him, so as not to get into any more arguments. Her eyes were drawn to the grace of Mac's movements. For a man of his height and build, his walk was truly sensuous though definitely very masculine.

He stopped by the open door to let her enter first.

'Ma'am,' he drawled, partly blocking her way so she had to brush past him to get indoors.

Acknowledging her thanks by way of a nod, as her throat was too constricted to utter a word from the unexpected physical contact with him, Laurel waited as he walked down the hallway.

'This will be your room,' he

remarked, opening the door and going inside.

While he checked to see if she had fresh bed linen and towels, she gazed around in surprise.

It was smaller than Jim's but was decorated just as nicely. The gentle shades of pink and lilac of the wallpaper and curtains, were echoed in the handmade quilt thrown over the brass-framed double bed, giving a definite feminine feel to the room. Already she was beginning to feel at home.

'We don't usually lock our doors around here,' he informed her, dropping her key on the quilt. 'My room's right next door if there's anything you need.'

'I'm sure I won't have to trouble you.'

'No, you already know where to find Jim,' he replied, his lips thinning.

Could she really put up with Mac's snide comments for four weeks? It wasn't as if she was used to mixing with men of his calibre. To be truthful, she hadn't had many male acquaintances in the past, mainly due to her mother. If she dared to bring a boyfriend home, they'd be interrogated to the point where Laurel wouldn't ever see them again.

'It's too easy to make a mistake,' her mother would tell her, refusing to inform her why she held this view. 'You have your life ahead of you, Laurel, to find Mister Right.'

In the end, Laurel had concentrated on her career as secretary to the Financial Director of a local engineering firm, until the recession brought down the company and she was made redundant. Now she was free to make her own judgements over jobs and men.

Her green eyes clouded from thinking of her late mother. Should she tell Jim the truth now and clear up the misunderstanding once and for all? This deception had already gone on too long.

Looking up, she confronted Mac's inquisitive stare.

'Before you go, can you tell me what's wrong with Jim? He hasn't said anything to me about his illness.'

'That's because he hates being treated as an invalid,' he replied then raised his brow. 'Why do you want to know?'

'I'm just curious, that's all,' she answered nonchalantly, adding a casual shrug of her shoulders for emphasis. 'There seem to be a lot of things you don't like him doing.'

'I'm only following his physician's recommendations to the letter. Pity Jim doesn't, and it's his health at risk, not mine.'

From the snippets she'd garnered, Laurel guessed what it could be.

'Is it his heart?' she prompted, hoping fervently that she was wrong.

She sighed heavily on seeing Mac nodding.

'He has tablets to control the condition,' Mac informed her, not noticing her concerned sigh. 'He's due to have bypass surgery in two months.'

'He's that bad?'

Again he nodded in agreement.

'Which is why he can do without any hassles or over-exertion. His illness isn't common knowledge among the staff. The only reason I'm telling you, Laurel, is because he seems determined to keep you around.'

It was too late to back out of her agreement now, she thought, sitting on the edge of the bed when she was alone. If she was to build up a friendship with her father then she'd have to go along with Mac's rules. Tears stung her eyes recalling the details of Jim's illness and impending operation. She'd just lost one parent — and now that she'd met her other, it seemed she could lose him, too.

Opening her handbag, she found the photograph she'd brought with her, the one which had sat on the mantelpiece since she was young. Until a few days ago, she'd thought the man at her mother's side was James Smith, her late father who'd died before she was born.

Her fingers traced lightly over his image. The photo hadn't lied but the truth had been corrupted by her mother. Details like he'd been born in Hertford, England, not Hartford, USA. She swallowed away the tight lump which had formed in her throat while pulling out the envelope containing her mother's letter. Unfolding the sheet of notepaper, she re-read it.

'Why didn't you tell me, mum?' she whispered as her eyes scanned her mother's scrawl, written, she guessed, in the nursing home weeks before her death. 'Why did you make me wait? Why did you let a stranger give this to me?'

She could hear her mother's voice reading the words.

Dear Laurel, I feel it's time you knew the truth. Your father didn't die before you were born. When I left him to return to England to be with your sick granddad, my father, he was running a ranch in Colorado.

53

*Our marriage wasn't a good one.
We both knew it wasn't going to last
but I fell pregnant with you and there
seemed no way out. If I'd waited and
we'd got divorced, your father would
have got custody of you because he
had money and could afford the best
lawyers. So I wrote and told him I'd
lost you after the arduous journey
home.*

Tears trickled down Laurel's cheeks.

*He believed me, darling, and he
agreed to a divorce so I reverted to
my maiden name Smith, the name
you were given at birth instead of
Richardson, Jim's name. Please try to
forgive me, darling. I couldn't have
stood to lose you to him because I
was told I wouldn't be able to have
any more children, though it's not a
condition that's hereditary.*

After the closing lines of apology and
of goodbyes, was the ranch's address.

It was as painful now as it had been hearing Mr Saunders reading out the letter in his office. He, too, had been surprised by its contents, having considered her mother a widow of many years.

Wiping away her tears, Laurel replaced the photograph and letter securely in the zipped compartment of her bag. She couldn't let them fall into the wrong hands. As far as her father was concerned, his child had been miscarried and Laurel was a stranger. It seemed she wouldn't be able to inform him to the contrary because his health was at stake, but at least she'd have a few weeks to be with him. It couldn't make up for the years when she'd been praying for a miracle, though it was the next best thing.

Luck had guided her to Jim on her first night in town. If only that same luck continued to hold, keeping Brandon McGuire away from her while she was here.

She guessed Mac was shrewd and

wouldn't be fooled by her act for long. If he was angry thinking that she was a gold-digger after a sick man's money, what would his reaction be when he found out she was Jim's daughter arriving just before his life-saving operation?

She began to shake.

No, Mac could never find out, but how was she going to find the inner strength to fight someone as powerful?

She got up from the bed, smoothing the neatly-sewn quilt and glancing around the room which might have been her own, if circumstances had been different.

What shall I do, she thought to herself. What can I do?

3

'Have you settled in?' Jim asked Laurel, when she appeared that evening, in the room set aside as a lounge for the guests. She glanced round cautiously to see if Mac was present.

'Yes, thanks,' she replied, sitting on the armchair next to his, in front of the unlit stone fireplace. Above it, was a stuffed elk's head whose unseeing glass eyes seemed to be watching her every move.

She averted her attention to her lap where she was entwining her fingers nervously over the floral cotton print of her dress.

'I'm sorry about earlier . . . about me and Mac.'

After a lot of soul-searching in her motel room, Laurel had decided to go ahead and move to the ranch, promising herself that if things became too unbearable, she'd leave.

'I know Mac can be headstrong but don't hold it against him.'

'You sound as if you're very fond of him,' Laurel murmured, gazing up into his face.

She hadn't known what her father would be like and was glad he had a kind temperament. If he'd been an ogre it would have shattered the dreams she'd built up.

'I couldn't wish for a more loyal friend, Laurel.' He smiled. 'He's the nearest thing I'll ever have to a son. When he used to come here on vacation, we'd go fishing together or ride up into the mountains. I swear that boy was born on a horse — Mac's a natural with them.'

'Didn't his family come from this area?' she enquired, taking a glass of wine from the drink tray Billy was proffering and inwardly reminding herself of her intolerance to the altitude. One glass would have to suffice tonight.

'A long way back,' Jim answered then asked Billy for a glass of mineral water. 'My diet,' he told her and went on, 'Mac's father still lives up in Denver. Brandon Senior's not interested in the outdoors. It seems to have skipped a generation. The McGuires have been around the area since old Patrick arrived from Ireland.'

'So he let his son come here for his holidays, alone?'

'There wasn't a lot for the boy to do in the city,' Jim explained. 'His mom died when he was eight and his father couldn't really cope with a growing son, but don't quote me on that!'

'I won't,' she remarked, feeling compassion for Mac losing his parents so young. For years, she, too, had felt that sense of loss, that something, someone, was missing in her life. But now her father was here. Mac could never be as fortunate. 'He was lucky you took him under your wing.'

'His grandparents loved him, too. They left Mac their share of the ranch and the area of land which Passion stands on, knowing he wouldn't sell off either of them to property developers, which his father probably would have done.'

Laurel toyed with the stem of her glass.

'Jim,' she said cautiously, 'you mentioned he's like a son. Haven't you any children of your own?'

He shook his head slowly.

'No. My ex-wife had problems. None of our children went full term.'

'Oh, I'm sorry,' she interjected, shocked by his revelation. She hadn't been the first.

'With her last pregnancy, it looked as though we were finally going to become parents.'

'And she lost that baby, too?' she whispered huskily.

'In England,' he replied, taking a long draught of water. He suddenly looked up at Laurel, his green eyes scrutinising her intently. 'Do you know, you would be of a similar age to my son or daughter. Maybe that's why I felt protective when I saw you sitting all alone at that table in the bar. You brought out my paternal instinct.'

'And I'm not the sort to go off with strangers. It's just that you reminded me of one of my uncles. He's a kind man, too.' A pink tinge coloured her skin.

'Do you have a large family back home?' he asked, and she wished he hadn't.

'The same size as most others, I suppose,' she answered casually, not wanting to get into deeper trouble. Any lies would have to be remembered. Even if Jim didn't seize on discrepancies in her story, she knew Mac definitely would. 'I forgot to ask, have you got another cook yet?'

'A friend is stepping in tonight and our new one will be starting in the morning. I'm hoping she will be as good as the last but not have as many tantrums.' He sighed deeply. 'He and Mac didn't get along.'

61

'What happened?'

'You can ask Mac yourself, he's just coming over.'

'Jim, Laurel,' Mac drawled, reaching them and sitting down on the armchair opposite her, crossing one leg over the other.

'Your usual, Mr McGuire,' Billy said, handing Mac a glass of amber liquid with lots of ice.

'Thanks, Billy.' He took a long sip then directed his blue gaze back to Jim. 'Could you oversee the arrangements at the stables in the morning? I've had some unexpected business come up. I'm going to be tied up for most of tomorrow.'

'Sure,' Jim replied. 'Maybe Laurel can help me. She's a hard worker and has fewer tantrums than Kenneth.'

'Then perhaps she should help the new cook for the next day or so,' Mac suggested, not acknowledging her presence. 'Have you been shown around the property yet?' he asked her directly.

'No,' Laurel replied through tight lips.

'If you're up early, I'll give you a quick tour. You should know the layout so you won't have to bother Jim unnecessarily for directions.'

Her mouth relaxed into a smile. He was doing his best to keep them apart.

'I couldn't put you to so much trouble when you're busy.'

Seeing Chantelle arrive in the room, wearing a dress that was more suited to a night in a disco than one in the ranch's lounge, she wondered what or who was going to keep Mac fully occupied. They were both attired for a night on the town. Was it a coincidence? She doubted it.

She didn't like the wicked smile that came to his full lips and which lit up his eyes.

'It'll be a pleasure, ma'am, and also an instructive half hour. Do you think you'll be ready to leave at seven?'

'Of course,' she replied, glad that jet lag would at last be an asset, and not a nuisance. 'We could make it earlier if you'd prefer.'

'OK, let's make it six-thirty. I'll be waiting on the porch.' Obviously sensing Chantelle's penetrating stare, he glanced around then got to his feet. 'I should mix with the guests before dinner.'

Just as she was about to give a sigh of relief because Mac was leaving them alone to chat, he stopped and added as an afterthought, 'Oh, and remember to wear something warm, Laurel. I wouldn't want you to catch a chill so you have to stay in bed for the rest of your stay.'

'I will,' she retaliated, noting his look which had gone from her to Jim then back again.

During the meal, Laurel sat next to Jim, but was conscious of Mac's presence the whole time even though he was at the far end chatting to Chantelle and her friends.

Feigning tiredness afterwards when Gary asked her to join him for a drink,

64

she returned to the tranquillity of her room and studied the cross stitch embroidery kit she'd purchased in town.

With the television on in the corner for company, she propped herself up on her pillows and began the picture of a pretty New England cottage. It would be a lovely memento of her holiday, she mused, and wondered where she'd be able to hang it when it was completed.

★　★　★

Laurel woke the next morning with a start. The heavy curtains blacked out any outside light. Quickly turning on the bedside lamp, she grabbed her watch and gave a sigh of relief. It was just before six o'clock. The effects of jet lag were subsiding, she thought, getting up for a shower in her bathroom then changing into her jeans. She glanced in the mirror on the back of the bedroom door.

Was there anything Mac could

criticise her for? Running a comb through her thick hair, she studied her functional clothes, resisting the urge to add a light coat of lipstick. She didn't want him to think she was trying to compete with Chantelle for his affections. Though she had to admit, Mac had looked so handsome last night.

Stepping out on to the veranda, she stared in awe at the scene that greeted her in the early-morning light. The sun hadn't yet appeared over the range of eastward mountains and the horses in the corral were dark, shapeless figures. Around her the birds' chorus filled the air.

What a lovely time of day, she thought, going forward to lean on the white wooden rail, her breath appearing as tiny, candyfloss clouds. Shivering, she wondered if she could pop back for her jacket. Mac had been right when he said she'd need to dress warmly.

A noise to the left of her made her jump.

'Beautiful, isn't it?' Mac's voice drawled.

She hadn't seen him sitting in a rocking-chair in the shadows. Coming slowly towards her, the wooden planks creaked beneath his sturdy, leather boots. Shivering again, she felt they were alone in the world. Her rash of goose pimples were catching on her pastel-hued angora, making her skin itchy.

'I'm not late.' She murmured her protest, her nostrils catching the faint aroma of his sensual aftershave. Its potent scent summoned up the impression of a boardroom, not of a corral.

As she stared up into his face, her senses reeled. What was wrong with her? Quickly she regained her composure, her spine stiffening.

'I didn't say you were,' he replied, the corner of his mouth lifting as he suppressed a smile. 'Don't you have a pair of boots with you, Laurel?'

'They didn't seem necessary on a touring holiday,' she explained hoarsely, her mouth dry from his steady gaze.

'We'd better get started,' he told her, striding across in the direction of the stables so she had to practically run to keep up with him.

If he continued at this rate, she'd be exhausted after ten minutes. Was he doing it purposely, to rile her or so she'd be too tired to be of help to the new cook?

A young man, similar in appearance to Billy, came out when Mac called to him.

'This is Billy's cousin, Dwayne,' he informed her then went on, 'Laurel will be staying with us for a short while.'

'Pleased to meet you, ma'am.'

'Are things ready, Dwayne?' Mac cut gruffly into the pleasantries.

'Just as you instructed, Mr McGuire.'

'Good. Take Laurel into the office and see if there's a spare pair of boots that'll fit her,' he ordered. 'I'll be waiting here.'

'What on earth do I need boots for?' she whispered to Dwayne when she walked with him to the small building.

'Trainers don't have heels which means your feet could slip from the stirrups.'

'Stirrups?' she cried in alarm.

'Unless you're counting on riding bareback, ma'am.'

As Dwayne sorted through the boxes stacked in a cupboard, Laurel slid into a chair, her quaking legs losing their strength. She prayed fervently he wouldn't find her size but unfortunately he returned with a pair that fitted perfectly when she pulled them on.

'You may as well hold on to them until you leave,' Dwayne remarked, watching as she got up and flexed her ankles in turn, while she hoped they'd pinch. But they didn't — they could have been custom-made for her.

'You've got a good morning for it,' Dwayne said enthusiastically. 'You'll find Fury doesn't live up to his name.'

'Wouldn't it be easier to walk, or go in my car?' she suggested, walking outside to where Mac was holding the reins of two huge horses.

'You're giving up the chance of a free ride?' he queried, patting the black horse's muzzle. The animal gave a sudden snort and shook his head. Laurel stepped back hastily. 'Jim told me you'd come here so you could ride. I thought we'd combine the two.'

Of all the times for Mac to be considerate to her. Reaching out slowly, she touched the silky black mane.

'Do you think he's gonna eat you?' Mac laughed.

Immediately, Laurel's proud streak surfaced and she held her head high.

'Of course not! I presume this is Fury?' she asked as Mac handed the reins to her.

Her fingers tightened over the leather straps, fear chilling her body. She had to tell Mac the truth. He was going to find out soon enough. Better to lose face now than end up on her bottom in the dust.

'Mac, I need — '

'Some help? Take my horse, Dwayne,'

he said, passing the rein to the young man then coming behind her.

'No, we need to talk,' she insisted.

'We can do that when we've got started. Put your foot in the stirrup, Laurel,' he prompted, then suddenly laughed. 'They must do things different over in England. Get up like that and you'll be facing his tail!'

'I never said I was an expert.' Her cheeks seared.

'So it seems,' he replied as she changed over. 'Push up and bring your other leg over his back.'

'Watch me,' Mac told her as Dwayne steadied Fury who was starting to get agitated.

Doing as she was asked, Laurel regarded Mac as he swung up into the saddle in one fluid, effortless movement.

Her attempt was inelegant in comparison, though she did manage to get up into the working Western saddle, clenching the pommel with her damp hands.

'Are you a complete novice?' he asked, bringing his horse around so he was beside hers, nodding when he saw her gripping on for all she was worth.

'Yes. Jim must've misunderstood me. I said I wanted to learn to ride.'

'Strange,' he murmured, appearing puzzled. 'Usually he has excellent hearing. Well, it seems as if I'll be giving tuition today after all.'

The ground seemed so far down as they began to move that Laurel deliberately concentrated on the horizon rather than on the horse beneath her. Within a few minutes, when it seemed Fury was to be trusted after all, her muscles relaxed although her fingers continued to grip the reins.

At Mac's command, his horse went into a trot and Laurel's followed across the field.

'Go with the horse,' Mac called out to her as Laurel bobbed up and down in the saddle.

Copying Mac's movement exactly, she felt less frightened, in fact she was beginning to enjoy it. The sensation of the breeze on her cheeks was exhilarating.

Suddenly, without warning, Fury snorted, shied away to the side then sped across the field as though the devil was after him.

'What on earth — ' she heard Mac shout out in annoyance while she clung to the pommel and Fury's neck.

'Fury, stop!' Laurel sobbed fruitlessly as he galloped onwards.

She was sliding to one side of the saddle, the ground coming closer by the second. Over the thundering beat of her heart, she could hear the sound of hooves catching up with her.

'Just what do you think you're doing, Laurel?' Mac stormed, reining her horse in to a halt then catching sight of her now blanched skin. 'What did you do to him?'

'Nothing,' she protested, easing herself into the middle of the saddle, her bottom sore from the pummelling it had received at Fury's top speed. 'He just took off!' she sobbed.

'Do you want to rest for a few minutes?' Mac asked, sounding surprisingly concerned.

'I've got to get off this horse,' she replied unsteadily, feeling her nerves had been cut to shreds.

'Wait there, I'll help you down.' Quickly he dismounted, letting his own reins fall but gripping hers while he spoke for a few moments in a low, calming voice to Fury.

This time, she didn't protest and let Mac guide her to firm ground. His hands lifted her down, gently lowering her on to the ground.

'I'll be fine now,' she proclaimed when he didn't remove his grasp. Her legs had turned to jelly and she felt grateful for his help, knowing if he let go of her, she'd fall to the ground. If she turned around she'd be in direct confrontation, she knew, but she felt almost embarrassed having to face him.

'He must've been spooked by something,' Mac told her, his breath warm

74

on her neck. It was far too sensuous, making something within her body burn with longing. 'Maybe a snake.'

Immediately Laurel shot around to confront him.

'A snake?'

She didn't know which frightened her more — snakes or her reaction from the touch of Mac's hands, which were fortunately by his side again.

'We do have them here.' He nodded.

'Is there anything else unpleasant around that I should know about?' Her eyes widened in concern.

'There are ticks, too — but fortunately you're wearing trousers,' he said, his eyes skimming over her jeans. 'You should check yourself for them if you've been out in long grass as you could get Rocky Mountain fever, which has been known to be fatal.'

'Are you trying to scare me?' Laurel breathed as his blue eyes levelled with hers.

'No. I'm just warning you of the possible dangers, as I would anyone else who isn't used to life in the mountains. And you're obviously not used to it.'

Side-stepping from his closeness, she conceded by giving a nod.

'I'm glad you've told me — we don't have things like this where I come from.'

Handing her Fury's reins, he went over to where his own horse was patiently grazing and returned with the animal.

'Would you prefer to walk back?' he asked, a small smile appearing on his lips.

Her body was still quaking but her stubbornness held firm.

'I'd like another try at riding, if you think I'd be safe.'

'I'll say this about you, you don't give up easily, do you?'

Mac waited beside her while she got her foot in the stirrup and she wanted to cheer out loud when she got up into the saddle at her first attempt.

'Well done! You're getting the hang of it,' he praised her as he swung up on to his mount and kneed against its sides to get it moving. Fury followed and Laurel tried to relax, but it was difficult after her recent scare.

'So where are you from — London?' Mac asked shortly, when she was beginning to feel in tune with Fury's movements.

'A small village north of there,' she replied evasively. Hertfordshire may ring warning bells in his head if he already knew a lot about Jim's past relationship.

'I'm surprised you've chosen to come here, Laurel. Usually British vacationers head for the attractions of sunny Florida or California,' he mused, glancing across at her.

'I have my reasons,' she answered which caused Mac to lift a questioning brow. She qualified it by adding, 'Mainly that I get bored just sunbathing on a beach and I hate crowded places. I'm a country girl at heart and the Rockies sounded ideal.'

'Where are you going when you leave

here?' he enquired, his horse nearing hers.

Taken by surprise, her cheeks burned.

'I ... er,' she stammered, not expecting his questions to catch her out, 'I was hoping you or Jim could enlighten me of the best places.'

'How long are you staying in the States?'

Silently cursing Mac's inquisitiveness, she replied, 'A few months. The company I worked for went bankrupt and I decided to treat myself before the worry of trying to find another job.'

'What work do you do?' Mac demanded, his tone suddenly turning chilly again.

'Until the firm folded, I was its Financial Director's secretary.'

'You're highly qualified yet you're willing to act as an unpaid kitchen hand?'

'As I told you just now, I love the country and I wanted to repay Jim's kindness,' she insisted.

'How much would you take to leave here today?'

'I beg your pardon?'

'You heard me, Laurel — how much money do you want?'

'I don't want money.'

Seeing Mac's thunderous expression, she guessed he was serious but she wasn't about to give in. Her muscles tensed. She had to see it through — even for another week.

'I don't want your money or anyone else's,' she persisted. 'And I intend to pay my way. If you let me know how much you want in advance for my rent, I'll give it to you later today.'

'Hold it, Laurel. First, let's see how you get on with your work this morning.'

She was pleased to see they were nearing the stables so she could get away from Mac, although she'd actually enjoyed riding Fury after all. Maybe one of the other men could give her some extra tuition in her spare time — that's if Mac gave her any. When they'd dismounted and she'd retrieved her trainers from the office, Mac accompanied her to the house.

'So you're not going to change your mind?' he asked, his hand catching her arm and pulling her to a stop by the veranda steps. 'It's not too late, Laurel,' he declared, staring down at her.

It must have taken her mother a lot of courage to write that letter. For years she'd kept her secret locked in her heart and regardless of all the rights and wrongs of the past, Laurel knew she couldn't turn away because of this man confronting her. She had to see it through — for all their sakes.

'I'm going to stay on, Mac.'

4

By ten o'clock, as Laurel sat down at the kitchen table with a much-needed mug of milky coffee, she felt she'd already done a full day's work. Having helped Jim to cook breakfast for the guests, she'd assisted Mrs Evans, the new cook, with the vegetables.

'I've just seen Mr McGuire outside,' the grey-haired woman informed her as she entered her new domain. 'He wants you to go along to his room.'

'Did he say what for?' she asked, taking another sip from her mug.

'I'm afraid not,' the woman replied, moving to the sink and washing her hands. Over her shoulder, she added, 'Don't rush, though — I said you'd go as soon as you'd finished the vegetables.'

'I wonder what he wants now.' She sighed. Mucking out the stables maybe or would it be another of his attempts to buy her off?

'I thought he told Jim he was going to be busy today,' she added, recalling last night's conversation; busy plotting ways to keep her and Jim apart.

'If he's working in his room, then it won't be ranch business,' the woman informed her, as she dried her hands on a towel.

Mrs Evans, Laurel had found out, had stepped in a few times when they'd needed assistance and had been a friend of Jim's for years.

'I didn't know he had any other,' Laurel remarked, surprised by the fact.

'Oh, yes. His father wanted him to join the bank but instead Mac set up his own business in Denver. Mac's an architect. His company designed the mall which has just opened in Colorado Springs.'

'Then why doesn't Mac live in the city?' she enquired as the woman brought her own mug of coffee to the table and sat opposite her. 'Surely it'd make more sense, seeing as his company is based there.'

'You obviously haven't got to know Mac very well yet,' Mrs Evans replied, glancing at Laurel. 'If it was anyone else we were discussing, I'd agree with you. But with all the modern communication systems, he keeps in touch with his personnel from here. If he needs to attend important meetings then he flies up. There's an airstrip just north of the ranch. You probably passed it on the way here from town.'

Laurel nodded on recalling it, though her mind had been on other matters when she'd driven past it — like how she was going to get on with her father.

'I'd better go and see what he wants,' she said, draining her mug. 'He's not the most patient individual I've met.'

Going down the hallway, she stopped outside Mac's room and took a deep breath for courage. Her hands were trembling but she clenched one into a fist and rapped on the door.

'Come in,' she heard him call out.

Taking another breath, she did as she was ordered. The room at the end of the building was much bigger than she'd been expecting. Mac was working by the window, directly ahead of her, at a drawing board.

As she entered, he glanced over at her.

'Take a seat,' he said, motioning with his dark head to the chairs set out in front of his huge, wooden desk. 'I'll be with you in a moment.'

Fortunately there was rock music playing from his stereo that she recognised and she listened to it while she waited. She considered nervously that this was like being at the dentist's.

'OK,' Mac remarked suddenly, swinging around on the high stool and reaching out, turned down the volume of the stereo. 'Have you finished helping Mrs Evans?'

'She seems to have everything under control,' she replied cagily on noticing his steady blue gaze.

'Good,' he said, standing up and

strolling over to the desk where he perched on its edge, towering over her. Laurel shrunk back into the padded leather. 'One of our cleaning staff has called in sick and as we're having a cook-out by the pool tonight I'll need you to help down there,' he drawled, regarding her all the while. 'That's if you don't mind.'

'Why should I?' she replied, holding his stare. 'I told Jim I'd help in exchange for staying here.'

'I wouldn't ask but the rest of the staff are rostered on to other duties. I can't spare anyone else to do it.'

From his expression, she guessed that was a lie. He was putting her to the test. If she declined, he'd tell Jim she was being unco-operative and he wanted her off the ranch.

'What is it you want me to do there?' she countered, succeeding in keeping her annoyance from her tone.

'Make sure the place is clean and tidy. It was done before the group arrived but I know some of them were there for a swim this morning before breakfast.' His lips curved into a smile. 'As we didn't get that far on the horses, you can follow me down in your vehicle. I'll show you where everything's kept.'

'I can see you're very busy. If you give me directions, I'm sure I'll manage on my own.'

'Oh, no, I insist. You're welcome to use the pool at any time, although I can't guarantee when you'll be able to go out again on horseback, as our full-paying guests get precedence.'

'I can understand that,' Laurel agreed, then her brow furrowed. 'Will I be invited this evening or should I go into town to eat?'

'It would seem odd if we sent one of our friends into town to eat alone. We'll be expecting you to dine with us and to join in with the entertainment afterwards,' he declared standing up. 'I have a call to make. I'll meet you outside in five minutes.'

Feeling his stare on her back as she

left the room, she was glad Mac couldn't see her expression. She'd do all of his chores without arguing if it meant he gave her time to get to know her father better.

As she tugged her black one-piece swimsuit from a drawer, she suddenly wondered whether her mother had lived here. It hadn't occurred to her until now. There was so much she wanted to find out. How had her mother met Jim? Where had they married — in the small church in town or in England? All her life she'd accepted her mother's glossed-over details as the truth. She longed to find out what really happened, but could she without giving herself away?

★　★　★

Easing herself into the Jacuzzi two hours later, savouring the warm, swirling water, Laurel wondered if it wouldn't be easier to take Mac's money and run after all. She'd mopped the floors so they were pristine and polished the dining tables until they shone. Even Cinderella was allowed a few minutes to ponder on the meaning of life, she smiled to herself, submerging her shoulders.

'Hi!' A voice cut into her dreamy state. 'Do you mind if I join you?'

'Gary, it's you!' she cried in alarm, thinking that once again, she'd been caught out by Mac. 'Of course I don't mind.'

Carefully coming down the tiled steps, he sat on the ledge facing her.

'Just what I need after a morning in the saddle,' Gary said, stretching his legs.

Laurel had to agree — and she'd only been on Fury for barely half an hour.

'I must've been crazy to let myself be talked into this vacation, Laurel.'

'So this is your first time?' she enquired.

'And the way I'm feeling now, it'll be my last! How those Pony Express guys fared, it sure beats me.'

'I'm certain you'll find it gets easier,' she replied, glad of the warm water on her aching back. The black material of her costume caused her to slip and for a second she was submerged in the small pool. Coming up spluttering for air, Gary's hand caught her and helped her to her feet.

'It hasn't been one of my luckiest days,' she explained, giggling.

'Really?' another voice demanded behind her, making her body become rigid.

'Hello, Mac,' she murmured guiltily, turning to confront his quizzical stare.

He was standing above them, his fingers splayed on his hips.

'I came over to tell you lunch is being served shortly,' he proclaimed, picking up her towel from the tiles and holding it out as she got out of the small pool.

Instead of passing it to her as she'd hoped, he wrapped it around her wet body from behind so she was encompassed in his bare arms. The action was extremely intimate and she wouldn't be able to escape without a fight in front of Gary, a deliberate ploy on his part she knew.

His hands travelled slowly over the towel, drying the goose-pimpled skin of her arms. Her entire body was quivering from his caress.

'Where are your clothes?' he drawled sensually into her ear. She shuddered from the warmth of his breath. He shouldn't be having this effect on her.

'In one of the changing cubicles,' she answered unsteadily.

'Then let's go.' Keeping his arm around her shoulder, he waved to Gary. 'We'll see you up at the house.'

Guiding her past the large pool, Mac remarked quietly, 'You've done a good job down here, Laurel.'

'So you were checking up on me. I might have known.'

As she stopped by her cubicle, he spun her around to face him.

'And I'm glad I did. What were you doing?'

'Wasn't it obvious?' Her lips tightened into a thin line.

'I know what I saw. Now I'm asking for your interpretation of the facts,' he snapped, his hand still on her shoulder.

'I did everything you asked me to do. I was having a much-needed soak,' she retaliated into the unfathomable stare.

'With Gary.' His fingers curled tighter.

'Yes, with Gary! I could hardly tell him to wait until I was finished, could I?'

'Laurel, I'm warning you to be careful.'

With supreme effort, she shrugged his grasp from her body.

'Regardless of what you think, I'm not interested in any man — Jim, Gary or even you!'

'I'm glad to hear it,' he drawled, suddenly smiling.

'But if I were, I think I could look after myself. I don't need you to tell me to be careful,' she countered, holding her chin up proudly.

'I'm pointing it out not to save your face but to safeguard the future of this ranch. Gary's been asking too many questions about you,' Mac explained.

'So?'

'So,' he echoed, 'this group have come from Washington DC. Chantelle believes your new friend Gary works in a government department. The man he's rooming with does. She went out with him once or twice last year.'

Quickly Laurel recalled what she'd said to Gary in the Jacuzzi.

'We didn't say much — he arrived only minutes before you did.'

'If you have to talk to anyone, whether it's to guests or our staff, please take care. One word in the wrong ear and we could all be in serious trouble. What would your family say if you were deported?'

'It won't come to that,' she insisted, avoiding his loaded question. 'When I'm not helping you, I'll keep myself to myself. If you don't need me this afternoon, I'd like to drive into town to shop for a few things.'

In truth she needed some time to herself to think, away from here and the close proximity of Brandon McGuire.

'Unless Jim can think of anything else, that's fine by me,' he answered, surprising her. 'Although I do have one favour to ask of you.'

'Which is?' She sighed.

'I could use your secretarial skills in the morning. I've got to take some plans to a meeting tomorrow and I need some notes to be typed. My own secretary's involved in one of our other projects and I don't want to interrupt her.'

Although she'd have to share Mac's room, it would be preferable being back at the typewriter than having to act as his charlady.

Seeing her nod in agreement, he smiled.

'It's a date then. I'll see you at dinner, Laurel.'

The rest of her day went smoothly. At lunch she was able to sit next to Jim, at the far end of the table from Gary. Then later in town, she was fortunate in finding a blouse to wear tonight with her new cords. Treating herself to a bottle of eau de parfum from the amazing assortment in the drug store, she headed back to the ranch with her purchases in a much more positive frame of mind.

Checking herself in the full-length mirror, that evening, she was pleased with the fit of her new clothes. Even if the meal was more formal than last night's, she wouldn't feel out of place.

Once she was completely satisfied with her appearance, Laurel made her way to the lounge where the others were congregating.

'Would you all like to make your way outside?' Mac called out from the door as she arrived in the room. 'Dwayne will be bringing the others down shortly if you want to wait for your friends.'

Letting the guests go ahead of her, Laurel followed slowly in their wake.

Mac caught her arm as she went to pass him.

'I'm glad to see you've dressed warmly. Why don't you ride up alongside me, Laurel? I feel I should look after you, seeing as Jim is already down at the cookout,' he explained, guiding her down the veranda steps.

There was a horse-drawn carriage waiting at the bottom, with Dwayne on the front seat holding the grey horses' reins. While another boy helped the guests into the back of the carriage, Mac leaped up beside Dwayne, holding out his hand to Laurel.

Settling herself, so she was far enough away from Mac's legs in case they accidentally brushed against hers during the journey, Laurel stared over the horses to the track ahead of them. As they moved along over the compacted dust, they were jolted when the wheels hit loose rocks.

The guests didn't appear to mind the old-fashioned mode of transport, judging by the laughter coming from behind her. Laurel gripped the edge of her hard seat with both hands to steady herself from sliding over to Mac's side.

The evening breeze was whipping up the dust when they turned off down a smaller track. While they were bumping along, Laurel tried to wipe away some dust that had got into her eye.

'Don't rub it,' Mac told her, glancing in her direction. 'You'll make it worse. Wait until we get there and rinse it out with cold water.'

Her eye was streaming now and she was glad she hadn't put on mascara otherwise she'd have had black streaks down her cheeks.

'Not far to go,' he remarked as she tried to stem the flow of tears with the back of her hand.

Laurel noticed the horses were already slowing, obviously used to the short trip.

Two ranch hands approached. One took charge of the horses while the other helped the guests down from the carriage. Mac leaped down and held up his arms to Laurel.

'You can trust me. I won't drop you,' he said, smiling as she edged along towards him. She found it difficult to balance with one eye closed and was glad when his hands gripped her waist and brought her safely down.

'If you all go through to the lounge, drinks are being served there,' he advised the group, keeping an arm around her waist to steady her. 'Laurel, you come with me.'

Instead of striding off at his usual pace, he strolled with her. Laurel was very aware of his body's warmth through his thick denim shirt until they reached the changing rooms off the pool. Letting go of her, Mac put a plug in one of the sinks and ran the cold water.

'Lean over and use your hand,' he told her before leaving her side. Although she managed to splash some water into her eye, it still felt sore as she stood up, water dripping from her face.

'Here, dry yourself on this,' Mac

97

insisted, arriving back and handing her a towel. With his other hand he carefully lifted her eyelid. 'Look at me,' he commanded her in an unusually soft tone.

Mac's head neared hers as he studied her bloodshot eye. His finger then pulled down her lower lid and inspected it.

'It seems OK,' he drawled, his lips now perilously close to hers. 'You have the greenest pair of eyes I've ever seen, Laurel.'

She quickly pulled away from him, partly out of embarrassment at his compliment and also because she didn't want him to compare her features and those of Jim's. Getting her lipstick from her bag, she added an unnecessary coat.

Pulling out the plug, he leaned against the sink and regarded her.

'I can understand why Jim and Gary are fighting over you. You're a very pretty, young woman.'

'And I've already told you, I'm not interested in either of them in that way.

I haven't come to America to strike up a relationship.'

His black eyebrows rose with disbelief and it riled her.

'For your information, I've come over here for a complete break.' Her bottom lip quivered as she continued. 'My mum died twelve weeks ago, Mac. I've been nursing her and I couldn't bear to stay in our old house alone. Now, doesn't that answer your questions?'

She saw from his expression he was shocked. He lowered his dark lashes.

'I'm sorry, Laurel.'

'It's not pity that I'm after,' she explained. 'I haven't had much of a social life in years and it's good to be able to make friendships again.'

'And I'm sorry I misjudged you, Laurel.' He gave a sudden beaming smile. 'Let's join the others.'

The delicious ribs and succulent steaks were cooked on large barbecues while another long table held the salads, deep bowls of hot jacket potatoes and assorted pickles and sauces. Music was playing while the guests dined at the smaller tables. Laurel was invited to eat with Jim, Mac and Chantelle.

Later, when the terrace was cleared and the tables drawn back to its outer edge, a country and western group began to play. As there were few women there, she and Chantelle were in great demand.

Pleased when the music slowed and she could rest her sore feet for a while, Laurel excused herself from the man who'd been leading her around the floor and returned to her seat.

Mac had just come back from the bar and set their drinks on their table. Before Laurel had the chance to sit down, his hand caught her arm.

'I believe this dance is mine,' he drawled, with a hint of warning.

'Just one because my feet really are sore,' she replied, not daring to annoy him as he had been friendly towards her during the meal.

Leading her to the empty floor, he

encompassed her now tense body with his firm arms.

'Relax,' he murmured. 'I'm not going to hurt you, Laurel.'

She slid her arms up his chest so her hands rested on his shoulders. Pulling her closer to him, they swayed slowly to the song of unrequited love.

'You know, I've been thinking,' Mac said, a thoughtful look on his face. 'I think it's time you and I got to know each other better.'

'What do you mean?' Laurel whispered.

'Until this group leaves, you and I will be spending a lot of time together.' She didn't fight him as his arms drew her back to him. 'Gary has been talking to Jim again. He's becoming far too inquisitive, Laurel.'

'But what can I do?' she begged against his shoulder.

'Accept my romantic overtures with grace.'

'You are kidding!' Accidentally she trod on his toes and mumbled an apology. 'With you?'

'Keep dancing as if you're enjoying it, honey,' Mac warned her quietly. 'This only has to be a front for when we're in company. I'm not asking you to agree to a mad, passionate affair.'

'Good!' she retaliated, glaring up at his smiling face.

'Of course, if I repel you that much, you could always leave.'

'You really are trying to get rid of me,' Laurel said, keeping to the slow rhythm. 'First you offer me money and now this. Mac, I'm not changing my mind. I've promised Jim.'

He caught her face in his hands and brought his lips down on her mouth. The contact barely lasted three seconds before he pulled away, yet it had her feeling as if she'd been branded indelibly.

'We'll continue this discussion later,' he told her as the music ended.

Feigning tiredness when she got back to the table, she quickly finished her drink and returned with Jim in his car to the main house. She was scared to be in Mac's company any longer than was necessary.

Everything inside was warning her to beware yet she couldn't forget the tenderness he'd displayed after the horses incident then later over her eye. She had never felt like this before. It was a peculiar sensation, she mused as she tried to settle down to sleep.

But sleep wouldn't come and eventually Laurel decided to get up for a drink.

She put on her wrap and walked down to the kitchen. On the way, she unlocked the door to let out Jim's ginger housecat who was miaowing loudly.

'Jim?' she queried, seeing him in the armchair, the back of his grey head towards her.

He shifted around and smiled at her.

'Couldn't you sleep either?'

Running her hand through her tousled hair, she perched on the arm of the sofa next to his seat.

103

'Not really, no. Are you OK, Jim?'

'I was just sitting here thinking.' Her father nodded.

'Do you mind having company? I'm wide awake now.'

'Of course not. Help yourself to a drink from the kitchen.'

Jim didn't want anything but Laurel poured herself a glass of cold milk then returned and sat on the sofa.

'It's funny how things come to you,' Jim mused. 'Things you'd forgotten.'

She sipped her drink without commenting.

'How are you getting along with Mac?' he suddenly enquired.

'Fine,' she replied, shrugging.

'I'm glad. Forgive me from being forward, but I think you're just the sort of woman he needs in his life. I realise this is only your second day here, and I don't know you very well and yet . . . ' He rubbed his chin thoughtfully. 'Years ago I met someone — she was like you, Laurel, in many respects.'

'Was that your ex-wife?' she

prompted gently.

He affirmed it with a nod.

'When we met in England and fell in love, I didn't tell her the whole truth, something which I bitterly regretted and have since then. I brought her out to Connecticut, letting her believe we'd have a regular family life.'

'And you didn't?'

'No. I had inherited my father's prosperous business and I spent long hours at the office, leaving Angie on her own to fend for herself in a strange environment. Although I decided to sell up and move out here, the rot had set into our marriage. I admit in those days in Connecticut, money played an important part of my life but I never made it clear to Angie that I'd have given it all up to keep her.'

'Didn't you try to tell her that?' she asked, sipping her drink nervously.

'In those days, I was like Brandon — too headstrong for my own good. It's only with an old man's hindsight, I can see the errors of my ways.' He chortled.

'I was watching you both tonight at the cook-out and he was like his old self with you. It was wonderful to see.'

'Why did he change?'

Jim rubbed his chest and grimaced.

'After he got married . . . '

Laurel hadn't considered Mac was already married and it shocked her yet now she was more concerned about her father's sudden ashen cheeks.

'Jim, are you all right?' she begged.

'Could you get the bottle of pills from my bedside table?' he asked, grimacing again.

Quickly she flew down the hall and into his room. There were two bottles there — both names of the medications were unknown to her. Scared Jim's life was in her hands, she ran to Mac's door and rapped loudly on it. When an answer didn't come immediately, she turned the handle and opened it.

'Mac! Mac! Wake up,' she cried, running across the darkened room to his bed. 'I need you. Now!'

5

The bedside lamp was suddenly illuminated and Mac rubbed his eyes with his hand.

'Laurel?'

'Mac, I need you now!' she insisted, grabbing his naked arm. 'Mac, it's Jim. He needs his pills.' The pills were chattering in the bottles she was holding out in her quaking hand. 'Which ones does he take?'

In a flash, Mac was out of the bed and grabbed the containers from her.

'Where is he?' he demanded.

'The lounge,' she breathed, close to tears.

'Get him a glass of water,' he ordered as he ran ahead of her.

She hurried to the kitchen and her hands were trembling as she filled a glass. Her father couldn't die! The cat was miaowing outside the door but she ignored its loud plea and hurried to her father's side.

Mac took the glass from her and held it to Jim's lips while he sipped it.

'Why all the fuss?' Jim remarked, staring at their shocked expressions. 'It was only a mild turn — nothing to worry about.'

Laurel's legs had become weak and she sat on the end of the sofa, her body quaking.

Mac crouched next to her father and looked at him intently.

'Are you sure I shouldn't call the paramedics?'

'In two months I won't need these pills,' Jim said. 'I only asked Laurel to get them for me because I became breathless — I'm all right otherwise.

Mac helped Jim to his room and Laurel was left alone to contemplate what had happened. Her body continued to quake uncontrollably. Jim might have made light of the situation, but he was still a very sick man. If only she could tell him that his beloved Angie had loved him to her dying day . . .

'What in heaven's name were you up to, Laurel?' Mac hissed angrily when he suddenly arrived in front of her.

She stared up through misty eyes to see him with his hands on his hips.

'Well?' he prompted, tapping his fingers impatiently.

'We were talking then he asked me to get his pills,' she explained.

'Talking? At four in the morning?'

The strain had taken its toll and tears began to pour down her cheeks.

'Think what you like,' she retorted through her now open sobs.

'Laurel — '

'Just leave me alone,' she cried, burying her head in her hands and trying to muffle her noise for fear Jim would hear her. The room was chilly and she couldn't stop herself shivering.

'Here, take this,' Mac said, his voice was nearer and held more compassion.

She raised her head to find he was seated beside her and he was holding out a paper serviette he'd got from the bar. Taking it, she blew her nose.

'Neither of us could sleep,' she said unsteadily. 'I had to get up for a drink. Jim was up, too. We were only chatting for a few minutes when — ' Her voice faltered as she cried again.

'Hey, he wasn't in danger,' Mac declared, his arm going around her shoulders and pulling her to him for comfort against his chest. 'He's said so himself.'

'I was so scared,' she admitted, savouring the touch of his fingers as they stroked her arm reassuringly.

'The first time it happened, it shook me, too. That's why I insisted on him visiting a specialist. Jim's been like my second father. He's a good man.'

'I know.' Laurel nodded, wishing her parents could have made up their differences instead of living apart in misery.

'You're a strange young woman, Laurel Smith,' Mac murmured, his deep blue eyes regarding her closely. 'Within two days of knowing someone, you're worrying yourself silly over their health. Though there's more to it than that, isn't there?'

Immediately she tensed and tugged at the short hem of her wrap. Surely he hadn't guessed?

'I don't know what you mean,' she faltered.

'Did you lose your mother the same way?'

Shaking her head, she explained her mother's illness and Mac listened.

'And I don't suppose I've helped matters any since you've arrived?' he contended, smiling.

'Not a lot.'

'You just happened to turn up at the worst possible moment, Laurel. I was wrong to make you the brunt of my bad mood.' He grinned apologetically. 'I hope you'll forgive me enough to help me later this morning. I'm really in a jam.'

'The typing? No problem,' she replied, taking his hand as he helped her up.

In silence they walked down the hall, Laurel feeling far more comfortable with Mac than she had done before.

As they said good-night she saw a new warmth in his eyes and she was almost sad to leave him.

For most of the night Laurel lay under her quilt wide awake. Her initial assessment of Mac had been so wrong when he'd come charging into the bar. He was capable of such tenderness, she mused, shivering as she recalled his embrace.

Another thought also struck her; he was married. Sitting bolt upright, she wanted to cry again, this time from frustration. Never had she met a man like Brandon McGuire and he was already spoken for!

She cursed silently, pummelling her pillows to soften them. As she fell asleep, she wondered why his wife wasn't here at the ranch with him. Maybe tomorrow she'd try to find out.

★　★　★

'I've worked on a similar machine back home,' she informed Mac when he showed her the word processor she'd be using. 'Give me a few minutes to try it out,' she added pulling out the chair and settling herself.

'I'll get Mrs Evans to bring some coffee — if you'd like some?'

'Yes, please,' Laurel answered over her shoulder and smiled. For a brief moment their gaze locked and Laurel's pulse raced. 'I'd better get on,' she said, deliberately turning back to the keyboard.

After coffee was served, she sipped it gratefully while Mac showed her the documents he wanted typed.

'If you can't understand my writing, call out. I've got to re-do this last sketch,' he told her, taking his mug over to his drawing board.

At first she found his presence to be a distraction yet when she got further into the document, becoming interested in what he had drafted out for his meeting, she forgot he was perched on his stool only feet away from her.

'How's it coming along?' he called over, some time later.

'One more page and I'll be able to print it off so you can check it.'

Coming over, he topped up his mug with fresh coffee. Standing beside her desk, he looked down at her and seemed amazed.

'That's quick work. How would you like a permanent position?'

'My services don't come cheap!' she joked, taking her eyes from the screen momentarily. 'What company perks would you be offering?'

'Free riding lessons?'

'Go on,' she parried, turning over the penultimate page and typing his final paragraph.

'Body massages when Fury throws you again?'

Hitting the save key, she cupped her mug as the machine whirred away.

'If he throws me again, after yesterday morning's fiasco, I doubt I'll ever get on another horse!'

'You'll let one minor incident put you off for life?'

'It still feels a pretty major one to me, Mac,' she countered, her hand going to her skirted thigh and rubbing it.

'I'll have you back up in the saddle, riding expertly in weeks.'

'That's quite a promise.'

'I like a challenge, Laurel.' His smile widened. 'Besides, I've dealt with stronger-willed women than you in my time.'

The remark cut to the quick as she recalled Jim's comment of Mac being married.

Matching his smile as he returned to his stool, she countered, 'I don't want to hear the sordid details of your private life!'

He laughed loudly before turning back to his sketch.

While Laurel waited for the printer to churn out the completed pages, she strolled around the office end of his room, gazing at the framed photographs and prints on the wall.

'Where is this?' she asked, having paused by a sepia one of an old town.

'Passion,' he said, glancing up from his board.

She studied the narrow street with its horse-drawn carriages and people who were in old-fashioned working clothes.

'Is this Passion, too?' she enquired, moving to the next picture.

'From a different angle,' he replied, coming behind her and laying a hand on her shoulder. 'It's been neglected over the years.' With his other hand, he reached out and pointed to the roof of one of the houses. 'You can see the damage that's been done.'

'It's such a shame. I love visiting old places. I've never seen a real ghost town before.'

'If you're interested, perhaps you can take a trip up there before you leave.'

'I'd like that very much,' she declared, smiling up at him. 'Do you have any other pictures of it?'

'Boxes full!' He chuckled, waving to his shelves. 'You're welcome to go through them later. Take them into the lounge if you want — the group are out white-water rafting today and won't be back here until later tonight.'

'I'll do that,' she said, going over to get her work from the printer's tray. 'Here you are.' She handed him the wad of paper.

'I'll be needing six more copies. You'll find binders in one of the drawers.'

Taking the report back to his desk, she watched him as he read through it.

'Great,' he proclaimed after she'd waited with baited breath. 'I should have this last sketch completed when the rest are collated. I owe you one, Laurel.'

How things change around, she mused happily while making sure the presentation of the documents was faultless. Mac had excused himself, having packed his drawings into a large carrying case. He was in the shower and she could hear the water running. Leaving the stack of folders on his desk, she headed outside to the shady veranda.

'Hello, Jim. How are you today?' she asked, sitting on the wooden rocking chair next to his. At least there was colour in his cheeks.

'Taking things real easy.' He reached over and patted her arm. 'Thank you, Laurel.'

'It's the least I could do,' she insisted.

'All the same, I'm mighty grateful. I know you and I made a pact when you came here, but this morning we've secured extra help so you won't have to spend your hard-earned vacation time cleaning up after our guests. Instead, Laurel,' he continued, 'you're welcome to stay here for as long as you want as our house guest. No work. No charge.' He smiled at her.

'Thank you, Jim,' she said, tilting her chair so it rocked to and fro gently as she took in the scene ahead of her. The horses were grazing in the late morning sun, appearing so graceful and placid from this distance.

'I'm not the one who deserves all your thanks. Mac was phoning around before breakfast to organise the rosters. Just let us know if there's anything you want.'

'How long will Mac be away?' Laurel's gaze returned to the corral.

'In Denver?' Jim stroked his jaw thoughtfully. 'Usually he stays over and catches up with his father while he's there.'

She leaned forward and spoke in a conspiratorial whisper.

'There is one favour I'd like to ask, Jim.'

'Name it.'

'As the group are out today, could one of the stable hands give me a riding lesson? Even if it's only for ten minutes or so just to show me the basics.'

'Sure, but I thought you enjoyed riding.'

'So Mac hasn't told you what happened?'

'Should he?'

Although grateful he'd kept the

119

details to himself, Laurel found herself relating the story to Jim.

'I gather you'd like this lesson to be done without Mac's knowledge?'

'Just so long as it doesn't make things difficult between him and his staff.'

'Then I know the person to do it, Laurel. The lads will be finished their chores by three. Meet me over at the stable at three fifteen. Firstly, you have to get over your nervousness because horses can sense how you're feeling. Once you've accomplished that, I'll get Dwayne to go through the basics.'

'This is where you've both got to,' Mac said as he came out of the house, clutching a leather briefcase and his art portfolio. He looked quite the business-man in his grey pin-striped suit and maroon tie.

'When'll you be back?' Jim enquired.

He shrugged.

'Hopefully by tomorrow evening. Dwayne has the yard under control and the buses are booked for tomorrow's excursion.' He looked at Laurel suddenly. 'You're on vacation and Jim's resting. When I return, I don't want to see any evidence that you've been doing anything too strenuous.'

With a final beaming smile, he strode towards the parking area and opened the door of his white sports car. There was a sense of loss within her as she watched its departing dust cloud becoming fainter as he approached the ranch's double-bar gate.

'Do you have anything planned other than riding?' Jim asked.

'Mac said I could go through the snaps of Passion in the lounge.' She had to keep herself busy instead of counting the minutes till he returned.

'Then why don't we go through them together? It's been a while since I've seen his collection. If we don't finish before lunch, we can continue later.'

Going inside with him, Laurel felt so happy. She was able to be with her father for as long as she wanted and she could also be near the man who was taking over her waking thoughts. Everything seemed to be working out at last!

★   ★   ★

By the end of the day, Laurel had learned more about Mac's Passion and had managed to stay on a horse without being thrown. After dinner, she excused herself and returned to Mac's room to find the photograph of an old Passion homestead which had caught her eye. She wanted to use it to make up a cross-stitch pattern of her own. It was something she hadn't done before.

The telephone next to his working area suddenly rang and Laurel eventually went over and picked up the receiver.

'Hello?'

'Who is this?' a young-sounding American woman enquired.

'Laurel.'

'Laurel?' the woman queried. 'Am I through to the BJ Ranch?'

'Yes, you are,' Laurel replied, perching on Mac's high swivelling stool.

The woman sighed impatiently.

'Can I speak to Mac if he's not too busy, Laurel?'

'He's not here but I can get Jim for you. May I ask who's speaking, please?'

'Mrs McGuire. Mrs Brandon McGuire.'

6

Laurel nearly dropped the handset in shock. This was Mac's wife and she was talking to her!

'I'll get Jim for you,' she breathed.

'Don't bother, Laurel. Is Mac on the property?'

'No, he flew up to Denver this afternoon for a meeting,' she replied.

'That's OK. He'll probably be coming over here later tonight. I'm sorry to have troubled you, Laurel.'

For minutes after she put down the phone, Laurel sat on Mac's stool, deep in thought. Was this one of those modern marriages she'd read about — where the husband and wife lived separate lives?

Replacing the photo in its box, she went to leave the room then stopped in her tracks. In matching antique silver frames on the dresser there were two photographs. She studied them closely.

They were of couples in wedding outfits — both brides in white with long veils. Although she didn't recognise the first pair, she immediately knew the second groom. Mac was a lot younger, though he hadn't changed much. Smiling at the camera, his arm was being clutched by a stunning brunette.

There was no mistake. Mac didn't wear a wedding ring, she mused despondently as she left the room, but not all men chose to.

Even if Mac did have an 'open' marriage, Laurel knew as much as she liked him she could never get involved with him now.

She didn't want to be part of a messy triangle. When he returned, she would avoid being in his company alone as much as possible.

★   ★   ★

The following morning, over breakfast with Jim, after the group had left for their trip into New Mexico, she didn't mention Mac's wife had called. She had come here to get to know her natural father and that's what she intended to do.

For the rest of the day, she was in his company either learning more about horses or sitting with him on the porch. He read a book while she sewed.

As dusk was falling, so were her hopes of Mac returning today.

'It's getting too dark out here to work.' She sighed, becoming restless.

Jim glanced up from his novel, his brow furrowed.

'Is everything OK?'

She nodded and smiled reassuringly.

'You'll have younger company when the others return soon. There's not much for someone your age to do here.'

'I love the peace and quiet. I've accomplished quite a lot today on my embroidery and I've ridden on Fury.'

'Laurel, regardless of what Mac said, you don't have to remain at my side the whole time! If you want a swim, drive down to the pool — you have time before dinner is served.'

She rubbed her eyes which were tired from working on the tiny stitches.

'Maybe I will. A few lengths might wake me up a bit.'

It was wonderful having the huge pool to herself and she did indeed feel refreshed from her ten lengths when she returned to the main house.

Lights were on in the guest quarters as she passed so she knew Chantelle and Gary's group had come back. Approaching the parking area, tension returned to her body. In her brief absence, the white sports car had also arrived.

Fortunately the lounge was empty and she was able to get to her room without meeting anyone — Mac especially. After rinsing her swimming costume she noticed that there was a wrapped parcel on her bed. Puzzled, she read the attached card.

With much appreciation, Mac.

Tearing off the silver ribbon and bow,

she undid the paper to find a gift set of her favourite perfume. She sat on the edge of her bed, her fingers tracing over the items and marvelling at his generosity. It was such a nice surprise.

'It was a lovely thought,' she told Mac when she joined everyone in the lounge half an hour later for pre-dinner drinks.

'I wanted to thank you for all your help yesterday, Laurel,' he said, a glint in his eye. 'My company has won the contract.'

'That's great news!'

'And I'm sure it had a lot to do with your presentation,' he insisted as Billy brought them their drinks.

'But how did you know it was my favourite?'

He tapped the side of his nose and grinned

'I have ways of finding out,' he jested as Gary and Chantelle approached.

'We were thinking of going into town later and wondered if you'd like to join us?' Chantelle enquired, noting the position of Mac's arm and raising a questioning eyebrow.

'Thanks, but Laurel and I are taking a drive up to Passion tomorrow after we've had an early-morning ride,' he explained. 'Laurel hasn't been there yet. If you have a word with Billy, he'll arrange the transport into town for you,' Mac told the now gloomy Chantelle. 'Perhaps we can come along next time.'

'What's going on?' Laurel whispered when the couple strolled away as dinner was being served. Mac's arm was still encompassing her slim waist. 'We haven't made any plans.'

'We have now,' he replied, drawing her aside so they were out of view from the dining area. 'Chantelle is a lovely woman but she's on the look-out for husband number three. The last two were rich and elderly so I'm surprised she hasn't made a beeline for Jim.'

'She seems OK.' Laurel didn't remind Mac that he had been all over the woman on her first night at the ranch.

'You can say that because you're a woman and she doesn't have you firmly in her sights. This way, if they consider we're an item it means we're both safe. You won't have Gary interrogating you and I can have some peace, too.'

Throughout dinner, sitting alongside Mac, Laurel wondered why he should be so bothered if he was already married. He only had to tell Chantelle that his wife was up in Denver — show her his wedding photo if necessary!

Although she wanted to stay and chat to Jim, she felt awkward with Mac being there. When she'd finished her cup of coffee in the lounge, she excused herself from them.

'I'll meet you on the porch at seven for your next lesson,' Mac said to her.

He didn't notice the exaggerated wink which Jim gave.

'And you'll need to dress warmly if we're going up into the mountains afterwards. It can be very chilly, even at this time of year.'

Sitting in bed, sewing her picture, Laurel was pleased her work looked a lot like the photograph of Passion she'd chosen. Spurred on with enthusiasm, she continued to work until she heard the others go to their rooms.

* * *

A hand was gently shaking her and as she came to the next morning, she was shocked to find Mac perched on the edge of the mattress.

'I thought you might want a wake-up call.'

'Oh — yes, thanks.' Laurel couldn't have been more surprised to see him but she appreciated the gesture nevertheless.

'I've made you some breakfast as well, so — '

'I'll be through to the kitchen in ten minutes — once I've got dressed.'

'Great,' Mac said. 'I'll just go and wait for you then.'

He'd made Laurel eggs and toast with coffee and she devoured them, glad she'd eaten something before she amazed Mac with her riding skills.

Once breakfast was over, donning the jacket she'd brought along, Laurel kept up with his long strides to the stableyard. She tried not to reply to Dwayne's grin as she pulled on the riding boots.

'Remember what I told you, Laurel,' he whispered conspiratorially when they headed outside. Dwayne took Fury's reins from Mac's grasp.

She saw the astonishment on Mac's face as Dwayne immediately passed them on to her. Putting her foot in the stirrup, she got on to Fury's back with no trouble. Mac shook his head then slid up into his mount's saddle.

'We'll take it easy today,' he murmured as they walked the horses out pass the corral. 'Let's try a slow trot,' he called to her and she stifled a smile.

Laurel kept up with him, staying

upright this time. The pace of the horses quickened until they were galloping across the meadow towards the river.

'Whoa!' he called out, reining in his horse and Laurel followed suit.

'What's been going on here?' he asked, standing beside her horse with his hands on the hips of his jeans.

Bringing her leg over the leather saddle, she dismounted with ease.

'I don't know what you mean!' she protested, although her eyes were twinkling mischievously in the early-morning sun.

'Now I realise why Dwayne was so eager to be on early duty today. Who else was in this conspiracy, Laurel?' Mac looked very confused.

Feigning innocence, she turned to face him.

'You're an excellent teacher, Mac.'

Quickly reaching out his arms, he started to tickle her under the arms of her jacket.

'Tell me!'

Although she couldn't feel his fingers, the notion of being tickled sent her into a fit of giggles. 'Please, stop!' she begged.

'Then tell me, Laurel.' His arms went around her waist and he drew her into him. As if in slow motion, she watched as his mouth came down on hers.

Tantalisingly, he coaxed her to respond. Within her, an unknown fire of passion burned and their kiss deepened in intensity. Her arms went around his neck, not wanting him to end this wonderful embrace.

Suddenly his wife's voice burst through her thoughts and she pulled away from Mac, leaping back a pace.

'This is wrong!' she cried, her eyes wide in alarm.

'Why? It's what we've both wanted — you can't deny it, Laurel!'

'It's just wrong,' she faltered, turning away. 'It shouldn't have happened.'

'Why, Laurel?' His hand grabbed her arm and he spun her to confront him. 'Do you prefer older men? Rich, older men whose health is failing?' he spat out.

How dare he think she was like that! Her hands formed fists at her side.

'Ones who aren't married!' she retorted. 'From what I've heard, you're not in that category, Mac. I spoke to your wife when she phoned the other evening.'

'My wife?' he queried. 'Why would she be calling me?'

'So you admit it then!' she said, not hiding her temper.

'Yes, I was married once, but why was she phoning me? I heard she was some place in the Caribbean with her new husband. What did she say to you?'

'She said she was Mrs Brandon McGuire. When I told her you were in Denver, she said you'd probably drop by to see her later.'

'Oh, Laurel.' He sighed, reached out and ruffled her hair. 'It was my stepmother. Don't you know my father and I have the same name? That's why I'm called Mac, to differentiate us. I may be many things, Laurel, but I'm not an adulterer. I've been divorced from my wife for five years.'

Laurel didn't know where to look.

'Hey, it's OK,' he said, pulling her into his arms and hugging her. 'I know I didn't make a good impression when we first met.' She looked up at him and smiled ruefully. 'But I want to get to know you better, Laurel.'

He kissed her again although she held back, scared of what it could lead to. Never had she felt so deeply for anyone before.

'Laurel, I swear you don't have to be frightened of me. I would never push you into a situation you didn't want to be in.'

Mac tilted her face towards him and kissed the tip of her nose.

'We should get the horses back to the stable,' he mused, reluctantly drawing away from her. 'You have a lot of work to do today.'

'Work?' Her eyebrows raised in puzzlement.

He nodded and spoke over his shoulder when he walked to his horse.

'I saw the needlework you've been working on — the house in Passion. Well, I'd like to contract some — it was fantastic and I believe just what's needed. You'll see why in an hour.'

★ ★ ★

From her low leather seat, Laurel regarded the steep road ahead.

'Damn,' Mac muttered over the music coming from the stereo. 'I should have brought the four-wheel drive.'

Slowly he negotiated the sports car over the unmade road, avoiding the potholes.

'We had one of the worst winters in living memory this last year,' he explained when they were on a better stretch. Beside them, a stream was gushing over the rocky bed. 'The snow's only just beginning to melt on the higher ground.'

Even Laurel could feel the temperature dropping as they were climbing. Noticing her shrug deeper into her jacket, Mac turned up the heater.

Counting her blessings silently, she noticed a partly-demolished building on the hill above the road.

'Nearly there,' he said, turning off the stereo. 'I'll show you around then we can have an early lunch.' She was glad — breakfast had seemed like hours ago. 'Afterwards, you can stroll around while I get on and assess what needs to be done this month.'

'That sounds fine.'

'I want you to get a feel for the place, Laurel. I'll explain to you later the proposition I have in mind.'

Although she had seen his snaps at the ranch, it hadn't really primed her for the view as they drove around the sharp bend and a lopsided painted sign declared, **Passion**.

Ahead, a narrow street lined with

dark, wooden buildings lay sleeping in the Colorado sunlight. It simply took her breath away and instantly she knew why this place had become Brandon McGuire's passion!

7

'It's beautiful!' Laurel enthused, stepping out from the car which he'd parked beside one of the houses, off the road.

'It sure is.' Mac nodded in accord with her words.

'But why would people want to leave here?' she asked.

Unlocking the padlock which was securing the house's front door, Mac pushed it and it squeaked open on its hinges.

'There were easier pickings elsewhere. The mining companies pulled out when it became too expensive to extract the ore and the inhabitants soon followed them. Buena Vista was the nearest town and by a mule-drawn wagon it was a day's journey away. Things then weren't as easy as some film makers make them out to be.'

Mac went inside the house and Laurel took a step into the musky darkness.

'I'll light the lamps later,' he called to her as she waited on the threshold. Setting down the picnic hamper, he rejoined her and slid his arms around her waist. 'Are you ready for the guided tour?' he quipped.

'Indeed I am,' Laurel replied, smiling as he hugged her before they set off.

His enthusiasm was contagious, she thought, while he pointed out the buildings which had been the saloon, the general store, the blacksmith's shop and people's homes. It was so quiet, she shivered at the spookiness she was suddenly feeling.

Putting his arm around her shoulder, he cuddled into her.

'I've known it to be a lot colder than this in summer.'

'It's not that — I keep expecting someone to walk out of a door at any moment! I don't think I've ever felt so cut off from humanity before. Even

141

when I'm alone at home, there are always people in the street or cars going by.'

'Then we'll take a detour around Passion's Boot Hill,' Mac said, laughing. 'It's not the nicest of places.'

'You've roused my curiosity now, Mac. What is it?' she asked, stopping in her tracks.

'The local burial ground. Not everyone had families who could afford to transport their bodies down to the church.'

'Can we have a look?'

'If you insist,' Mac said. He guided her up the street to a patch of ground, encompassed by rusting railings. Threading slowly through the grey stones, Laurel noticed the epitaphs on some which hadn't been worn by the elements.

'It sounds as though it was a wild town,' Laurel proclaimed.

'Like most others around here. The men had money to burn and they spent it on whisky and women. Things calmed down when families began to settle.' There was a twinkle in Mac's eyes. 'I guess my great-grandpa got into some scrapes, too, before he got married.'

He took her hand and guided her back towards the street.

'What about your family, Laurel?'

'We're not interesting like yours,' she flustered. 'I've lost track of the where-abouts of my aunts and uncles.'

'You never mention your father,' he remarked.

She came to a halt and stared at the stony ground.

'My mum and dad parted before I was born,' she replied, taking care over her choice of words. She felt Mac might be able to tell if she was lying. 'Mum had to act as a mother and a father to me,' she explained, now daring to confront his gaze.

'It must have hit you hard when you lost her.'

'It has.'

'So you don't have anyone to rush

back to in England?' His hands went to her shoulders.

'No-one.'

'Good, then you'll be here long enough to fulfil the terms of our contract for your needlework?' he quipped, although from his tone she knew he wanted her to remain, to be with him.

She pinched his arm playfully.

'You work far too fast for me! We haven't sorted out the details and I haven't signed on the dotted line yet!'

'Then I'll have to win you around over our lunch.'

On a patch of grass behind the house, Laurel set out the tartan blanket while Mac brought out the picnic hamper. Inside were sealed bowls and she was surprised to find a feast of fresh prawns, smoked salmon sandwiches, salad and slices of asparagus quiche.

'What's this?' she declared when Mac pulled out a bottle of champagne and two glasses wrapped in linen serviettes from the basket.

'We have to toast our new partnership,' he said, undoing the foil and popping the cork. Quickly she held the glasses out to stop the champagne spraying too much.

Sitting down, Mac joined her, stretching out his legs. He touched her glass with his, then leaned forward and placed a kiss on her lips.

'Do you always negotiate business deals like this?' she parried, leaning away from him and smiling.

'Not often enough!' he said, grinning. 'Let's eat. You might be more compliant with a full stomach.'

After they'd eaten, Mac told Laurel he'd like her to base some needlework designs on the houses of Passion. He'd already recognised the one she'd been working on at the ranch and had loved it.

He informed Laurel of the amount of money he was prepared to pay her for ten pictures and she was stunned.

'Are you sure?' It was a good deal more than she'd expected.

'You're supposed to haggle and ask for more,' he told her, topping up her champagne glass. 'As you're obviously a novice, Laurel, let's say you'll be given that amount when you deliver them and I'll pay up front for the materials you'll need. Do we have a deal?'

'Absolutely! I really don't know what to say.' She tapped his glass with hers.

Having packed away the hamper, Laurel took a clipboard, paper and pencils from the boot and sauntered around deep in thought, making notes of things she wanted to add to her designs. Feeling slightly light-headed from the champagne, she hummed as she worked.

She no longer felt uneasy; she was here with the man she loved and no ghosts from the past could put a damper on her happiness.

A hand touched her shoulder when she was sitting on the boardwalk and she glanced up to see Mac studying her notes and sketches.

'You're left-handed.'

She nodded, wondering why he'd mentioned it.

'Jim is, too.'

'Is he?' she countered with nonchalance. Mac sat down next to her and pointed across the street.

'That's the building you've started sewing.'

'It's very quaint.'

'Like your English accent, Laurel. Would you like to see inside? The structure has been shored up so it's quite secure. The workmen are beginning working on some others next month,' he explained as she walked alongside him.

She followed him after he'd undone the padlocked door and went inside. Stepping over the threshold, she found it was a large basic room like the one in the first house they'd visited.

'All of my great-grandparents' children were born in here.' His deep voice echoed off the wooden walls.

No wonder there had been so many

photos of this place — the McGuire home.

'How many children did they have, Mac?'

'Eight.'

From the light coming through the dusty window and door, she gazed around in amazement, trying to work out how ten people could share this small area.

Catching her expression, he smiled.

'I like the idea of having a large family but not until I'd been married for a while.'

Not wanting to get into this particular discussion, she glanced at her watch. It was already two-thirty.

'I should get on,' she told him. 'I've a lot of stuff still to do.'

Immersed in her sketches, she caught sight of Mac once in the distance and waved to him. When it began to spit with rain, an hour later, she pulled up her jacket collar and stood under the wooden awning of a house which jutted over the boardwalk.

Before she knew it, the rain was coming down like ramrods and was bouncing forcefully off the formerly dusty street.

Worried now, she looked down the road where Mac was beckoning to her from his grandparents' old house. Threading her way down, trying to keep her back to the buildings so she wasn't soaked by the deluge, she shivered as a bolt of lightning crackled and lit the street for several heart-stopping seconds. She counted aloud. One thousand, two thousand, three thousand.

The boom of thunder echoed around the mountainside and she threw her free hand to her ear.

'Laurel, come on!' Mac shouted to her from the open doorway.

Tucking the clipboard inside her jacket and zipping it up, she took a deep breath for courage and ran as fast as her legs would carry her. Panting, she arrived in the front room, her lungs fit to burst.

Mac had lit a gas lantern and was peeling off his soaked jacket.

'I'd do the same if I were you else you'll get a chill,' he advised her.

She glanced down and her jeans were almost indigo from the knees down.

'There's a portable gas fire which I'll get out so they'll soon dry.'

In the now-lit room, Laurel noticed there was an old sofa in one corner. Mac was busying himself with the contents of a large box. He drew out a sleeping bag and brought it over to her.

'I only have one spare pair of jeans here. If you take off yours, you can sit in this.'

A pan of water was put on a butane gas ring, as she peeled off her soggy jacket. Mac was now connecting a large gas bottle to the small fire and his wet clothes were slung over the back of the only upright chair.

'You're well prepared,' she remarked, moving so she was standing behind him.

'Jim gave me good survival training

when I was young,' he replied, striking a match and holding it to the pilot light. 'I keep the basic necessities up here. Sometimes I come for several days if I don't have ranch or other business commitments.' The fire's flames were golden now and he took Laurel's jacket from her, laying it on the floor. 'Now your jeans.'

Going to the sofa, she sat on the edge and undid the zip, noticing Mac was purposely keeping his back to her. Quickly she tugged them off and pulled up the quilted sleeping bag to her waist.

'Thank you, Mac. I'm feeling warmer already,' she said, flexing her toes in the padding.

'Good,' he replied, towering above her. 'I couldn't have you sitting around freezing to death.'

She watched him while he made mugs of black coffee, one of which he handed to Laurel.

She cupped it, welcoming the heat on her skin.

'When do you think the storm will stop?'

'Difficult to say. We're gonna have to wait until it eases up though. It would've been fine if I'd borrowed the Jeep. But I don't want to chance our luck on the road at the moment.'

'Are we going to be marooned up here for days?'

He stroked her arm reassuringly.

'I'm pretty sure we'll be out of here by tomorrow at the latest. Don't worry, we won't starve — there are cans in the cupboard so we can rustle up a dinner and breakfast.

'I'll treat you to a meal in town when we get back. If you could order anything now, what would you have?'

'I'm not a fussy eater — I like most things.'

'You must have a favourite, Laurel,' he said, sipping his drink.

'OK, well, it's highly unsociable and not very good for you but I adore garlic bread which is piping hot and dripping in butter.'

'Mmm, sounds good to me. Do you like ribs?'

While they went through their ideal menus, she found they had very similar tastes and as the conversation turned to her hobbies, she learned Mac shared her love of art.

'My father wanted me to follow him into law but I dug my heels in. Eventually he relented and I studied architecture at the University of Colorado.'

'You were lucky.' She explained how she hadn't been as forceful with her mother and had kept her creative talent as a hobby.

'You're an excellent secretary. I'd have you work for me any day,' he said, smiling at her. 'Although your heart is obviously elsewhere and I'm glad I've been able to offer you the chance to fulfil your dream.'

She snuggled into the sleeping bag. 'Tell me more about your family.'

He shook his head in amazement. 'Do you know Laurel, you're an expert at passing the buck? I hoped that being here with you, I'd find out more about you.'

'There's not a lot to tell. I haven't led such an exciting life as you have. You've been around the world, visiting places I've only read of. You've got your own company in Denver and have shares in a fantastic ranch.'

He swivelled around and sat up against the wall, pulling his knees up.

'So? It hasn't automatically brought me happiness. Come on, Laurel, tell me: what has made you feel most proud?'

'Being able to ride well on Fury this morning.'

'No, that's too easy. I'm being serious.'

'And so am I! Jim and Dwayne didn't realise what they were taking on when they agreed to — ' She winced, realising she'd given the game away.

'I'd already guessed whom you'd coerced into your plan. They're good horsemen.'

The two of them chatted easily and as the hours passed, the storm died out, although the rain continued.

'Your jeans should be ready to wear,' Mac said, stretching and getting to his feet. 'You can help me get something to eat. I'm ready for anything.'

When Laurel was dressed, she stirred the pan of soup on the ring while Mac was sorting out their main course.

In a companionable silence, they ate their meal on the floor in front of the fire, balancing their plates on their laps.

Using water from one of the flagons which they heated on the single ring, they washed up the crockery in a bowl. Afterwards, Mac checked outside the door.

'It's stopped now,' he called to her.

'Really?' she answered, stacking the plates in the cupboard. She tried to sound more enthusiastic. Soon they'd be back in the real world and back at the ranch things would return to normal between them.

Joining him at the door, he slid his

arm around her shoulders.

'Our troubles mightn't be over yet, honey.' He sighed, hugging her.

'Why not?' She stared into the blackness.

'If we try to get down in the car now, we might become stuck halfway and it's a long walk back here. The storm will have flooded the stream and parts of the track might be washed away.' Mac turned to her. 'We can try if you want.'

'Do we have any other options?'

'If you're prepared to wait until tomorrow, it'll be easier in daylight as we'll be able to see where we're going. One false move tonight and we could find ourselves in a lot of danger.

'The water level should have gone down by then, too.' He ruffled her hair. 'Don't worry — if we're not back at the ranch by lunch-time, Jim will realise something's happened and will send one of the men to find us. He knows I've got an important meeting planned for late tomorrow afternoon in Denver.'

'Another one?' she enquired and he nodded.

'The other day the company agreed to my designs but tomorrow we'll be signing the contract. Two deals in one week is pretty good going, don't you think?'

'Two?' she countered, then remembered their own. 'I haven't signed anything to say I'll do it yet.'

He kissed the tip of her nose.

'I'm trusting you not to go back on your word, Laurel. So, shall we stay here?'

From his tone, she knew it wasn't really a question. The consequences could be disastrous if they left before daybreak.

'It's probably best,' she replied with resignation and he closed the door then went to make another hot drink.

She had wanted extra time with him but now she had it, she was scared knowing they'd be spending the night alone. Her body trembled recalling the passionate embraces they'd shared that morning by the river.

She longed to feel his arms around her yet she was frightened of committing herself fully to him, even though she knew she was in love with Mac. His emotions might not be running as deeply as hers.

Perhaps it was best if she brought up the subject of their sleeping arrangements now.

'Mac.' She breathed unsteadily, going over to where he was making their drinks. 'There's something we should discuss.'

'Yes?' His blue gaze turned on her.

'Who's going to sleep on the sofa?' She felt herself blush profusely.

'You will, of course! What kind of man do you think I am?' he replied most seriously but then beamed at her. 'I'll take the sleeping bag and sleep on the floor.'

'Are you sure?'

'Hey, if I was the chauvinist you accused me of being the other day, I'd have already made a claim to the most comfortable place,' he declared over the rim of his mug.

'I was rather rude to you. I didn't know what you were really like.'

They moved over to the sofa and sat on the edge. Mac slid his arm around her.

'How could I have thought you were anything like Anna?'

'Anna?' she queried tenderly.

'My ex-wife.' He retracted his arm and held his mug in both hands, staring down at the black brew. 'We got married just after I left college. Her parents were friends of the woman my father had just married — the woman you spoke to on the phone.

'On the face of it, Anna and I seemed to be a perfect match. We were from a similar background and she'd known how to entertain the clients I was hoping to bring into the new company I'd set up with my father's financial assistance.'

He sipped his drink and continued to avert his gaze from Laurel.

'Since then, I've repaid him in full. The company took off as I secured some major deals. What I didn't realise then was that my father-in-law's business was foundering. Instead of wanting to help her father out, Anna was looking for someone to pay her bills so she could carry on living the good life. To her, love had never played a part in our relationship.'

'What happened?' Laurel murmured, touching his arm reassuringly.

'We'd only been together several months when her motives became evident. She was incredibly calculating and out for every cent she could get. My father sorted out the legal mess her father was in so he didn't have to sell the family mansion. He then sorted out our divorce litigation.'

'Did you love Anna?'

'No, I don't believe I did. She's stunning and I was attracted to her, yet there was nothing in here,' he said, putting his hand on his heart over his shirt. 'Beneath her glitzy façade, there was little emotion for her to share with anyone. Just so long as she could drive her Italian convertible to lunches with her friends at the country club and enjoy the comforts of our penthouse apartment in the city, she was content. Nothing else mattered.'

Taking her hand from his arm, he threaded his fingers through hers.

'That's why it's been a welcome change to meet a woman like you.'

'I like you for who you are, Mac, not what you own,' she challenged him bravely.

'I've learned more about you today, Laurel, than I ever knew about Anna.'

'Maybe it's fortuitous we were caught here in the storm.'

'No, I believe we'd have gotten together sooner rather than later. When I was up in the city, I couldn't stop thinking about you. I wanted to get you something, not only as a thank-you gift for your work though I didn't want you to think I was trying to buy my way into your affections.'

'The set was lovely.'

'I recognised the perfume when we were dancing at the cook-out.' He smiled.

They talked long into the night and Laurel had never felt so comfortable with anyone before. But at the same time it was a strange feeling — knowing that she'd be quite happy always to be with Mac.

It took a long while to settle but she still awoke when the first shaft of the dawn's light came through the uncurtained window. Stirring, she found Mac was propped up on his pillow on his elbow, regarding her.

'Good morning. Did you sleep well?'

'Not too bad at all, considering.'

'I'll make some coffee then we can get going.' He noticed her sad gaze. 'If I could put off this trip to the city, honey, I would. We'll be together afterwards.'

She was pleased he considered them an item, yet she was still worried if and when she should mention her father's identity. Having made their drinks, Mac returned to sit on the edge of the sofa.

'I want you to listen to me, Laurel.' He set his own mug on the floor and turned to face her directly. 'I'm telling you this now in case you thought I wasn't being truthful last night.

'At the ranch I was plain jealous that something was going on between you and Jim, though I wouldn't admit it to myself. Honey, I hardly know you but I do know what I'm feeling here.' He put his hand over his chest.

'You asked me if I loved Anna and I can say quite truthfully that no, I didn't. In my life, I've never felt what I'm feeling for you at this moment, Laurel.'

Her mouth fell open in shock. She searched his expression for a sign he was joking. Mac remained serious.

'It's been less than a week since we met, I know, and I'll give you all the time in the world to reply.'

She could guess what was coming, yet she still wasn't prepared for hearing his words spoken aloud.

'Laurel, will you marry me?'

8

Laurel didn't know whether to laugh or cry. To say she was surprised by his proposal was an understatement.

'I'm not expecting you to answer me straight away, honey, but nothing has ever felt so right before.' Leaning forward over the sleeping bag, he brushed her lips with his. 'I love you, Laurel.'

'I don't know what to say,' she murmured, in shock. 'You told me you liked me but I didn't think you'd be proposing marriage.'

He took away her untouched mug of coffee which was getting cold then grasped her hands in his.

'I want us to be together. I want to show you how much I really do love you.'

'I can't quite take it in.' She shook her head and laughed nervously.

'I've laid myself bare. You know how I feel. Think about it then reply.'

'You're sure you don't mind waiting, Mac?'

He shook his head emphatically and smiled.

'Not in the least. It is a big decision to make. You'd have to move over from England, from everyone you know and start afresh.'

Passing her mug back to her, Laurel drank its tepid contents gratefully because her mouth had gone bone dry. She was being offered the chance to live with the man she loved and with her father! In her wildest dreams, she'd never expected anything like this to happen.

The cautiousness her mother had instilled in her was now making her hesitant. It was a major step and she should wait at least until his return from Denver until she told him she loved him, too.

Laurel took one last look around the old town while Mac packed everything into the boot of his car. Joining her in the middle of the street, he slid his arm around her shoulders.

'We can come up here anytime when I'm not tied up with one of the businesses,' he said, hugging her. 'You should be aware I work pretty long hours at times though I hope you'd accompany me if I have to spend the night in Denver or elsewhere.'

'If I was your wife, I'd want to do some kind of work.'

Steering her towards the car, he replied, 'First, you have our needlework contract to complete. Then it's up to you, honey. I'm not opposed to having a working wife so long as we can have some time to ourselves.

'If you'd like a studio, there's plenty of space over the stables which isn't being used and could be converted.' He smiled down at her. 'If you agree, I'm gonna have to find another location on the premises for my office.'

The excitement was overwhelming as she got into the car and strapped herself in. Should she wait or tell him now of her decision?

The first section of the downhill track was fine, although the stream was running fast, sometimes lapping over the gravel at the side. Mac was driving carefully and concentrating hard as they wound down the tight bends.

When they reached the point, over midway, where the stream crossed the road, he brought the car to a complete stop and tugged on the hand-brake. Getting out, he went to assess the damage while Laurel watched him with growing concern as he kicked the rocks with his boot.

'Get into the driver's seat, Laurel,' he ordered her on returning and opening her door. Undoing her belt, she got out.

'What's up?'

'I want you to put it in first and come slowly towards me. I'll indicate to you which way I want you to turn.'

'Wouldn't it be easier if you drove?' She hadn't taken the wheel of a sports car before.

'No. I may have to put wood under the tyres if they stop gripping.'

This didn't instil confidence in Laurel. There was a sheer drop barely three feet away where the water was disappearing over the rock into another larger tree-lined river way below.

'Get in but don't start her up until I signal to you.'

Waiting, she gripped the wheel with hands which were becoming moist from her rising nerves, watching as Mac hurried around collecting bits of timber from the hillside. She held her breath as he slid the last few muddy feet to the road and was glad he caught his balance in time.

'OK, Laurel,' he shouted and she turned the ignition key, firing the throaty engine.

'Slowly forward,' he yelled above its din.

Mac was on the other side of the ford and he beckoned her towards him. Putting it in the lowest gear, she yanked at the stiff hand-brake and depressed the accelerator. The car reacted immediately and she eased her right foot.

'This way!'

The rear offside tyre was spinning but stopped as she turned the wheel in Mac's direction. The chassis shook when the front ones hit the damaged track. The rear tyres also bumped on to the section and Laurel stared ahead.

In seconds, the front wheels were once again on firm ground and as the back ones joined them, she expelled the lungful of breath she'd been holding in with a loud sigh.

'You OK?' Mac hurried to her door and opened it.

'Just about,' she replied shakily and let him help her out of the low seat. 'I wouldn't want to do that again!'

'I'm gonna have to give you a lesson in the four-wheel drive. Even in the valley in winter, I can't always use this one.'

Getting back into the passenger seat, Mac was smiling over at her.

'We should do something about

getting your rental car back. It's crazy hiring it when you can use one of ours.' He shrugged his shoulders. 'We can discuss it at length after but you'll need wheels of your own eventually.'

'I haven't said yes,' she reminded him with a twinkle in her eyes.

'But you haven't said no, Laurel,' he said, starting the engine. 'So I guess the odds are currently stacked in my favour!'

'I promise you'll have your answer when you get back from Denver. Now there are a few things I want to ask you so I can plan which of the pictures I should finish first.'

During their drive to the ranch, they chatted and she knew Mac was going to be a wonderful, caring husband, despite her first impressions of him.

After turning off the engine, Mac came around and held her hand while she got to her feet then enfolded her in his embrace.

'I love you, honey,' he drawled sensually against her lips before kissing her passionately. She responded eagerly, heartbroken that they'd be parted for a few hours.

'You're everything I've ever wanted in a woman. You're loving, compassionate, as well as beautiful,' he murmured to her, as their bodies remained entwined. 'I want to share the rest of my life with you, Laurel, and that's no empty promise.

'I just wish I'd met you sooner, honey. I'd forgotten women like you existed, ones who don't have ulterior motives.' He hugged her again, thankfully not noticing the frightened expression which came to her face. 'The second time around is gonna be very different.'

Giving a noncommittal murmur against his chest, she savoured his touch on her body. Tears pricked her eyes as she thought about how much Mac would hate her when he found out that she'd been living a lie.

He'd said he hadn't loved Anna and it had taken him five years to recover.

What ferocity would she have to confront?

'Hey, what's up?' he asked when she clung to him. He lifted her chin. 'I'll try and get back tonight but I can't give you any guarantees.'

'I'm going to miss you, Mac,' she whispered, holding her sobs at bay.

'I'd ask you to come with me but it wouldn't be much fun. I'm gonna be stuck in a meeting for hours then I have to see my father. I wouldn't wish my stepmother on you, not just yet anyhow,' he added with a deep chuckle. 'Tomorrow evening I'll take you to dinner and we're gonna order everything we dreamed of last night in Passion, OK?'

She nodded as she let him lead her to the front porch.

Stopping at the threshold, he beamed down at her, holding her hands in his.

'I have to get ready now but I'll book the table and tell them to have the champagne on ice.'

'But — '

Her sentence of doubt was cut off by a final kiss. With a ruffle of her hair and a chuckle, he was gone.

Instead of following him inside, Laurel walked dejectedly to the paddock fence and rested her arms on the top rail. Through the thick mist, she sobbed quietly while the shape of Assunna approached her.

'Hello,' she murmured, stroking the old mare's soft grey muzzle with affection.

The horse snorted then bent to graze as she realised Laurel had no carrots or apples for her.

'I've heard you had quite a night,' Jim's voice proclaimed behind her and she hastily wiped her face with her hands. His brow creased when she turned around. 'What's up, Laurel?'

'Oh, I'm just tired and things have got to me now. I'll be OK after a shower and a few hours' sleep.'

'How did Mac react when he saw you riding? I didn't see you before you left yesterday.'

'He was very surprised but wasn't annoyed we'd set him up,' she replied lovingly, then sighed. Was it only yesterday?

'I did tell you he was a good man when you got to know him,' her father insisted, a wry gleam lighting his green eyes.

'Are you attempting to matchmake?' she countered, trying to sound light although her heart was feeling heavier by the moment.

He chuckled and put his arm around her as they strolled back to the house.

'Is there any need? I may be getting older but I can still read the signs, Laurel. I was exactly the same when I met Angie.'

Feeling unable to control herself much longer, she replied with a wistful smile, 'I'll see you later.'

Hurrying to her room, she locked the door after her then sped to her en-suite shower room. Turning on the taps, she leaned against the sink and began to cry openly, knowing no-one would hear her above the noise of the shower.

How could she stay here? Wasn't it better that she remembered Mac's loving side of his nature than the ferocity when he learned she'd been living a lie?

She wouldn't have the inner strength to keep her parentage a secret from him for ever. While it existed, there'd be a mighty chasm keeping them apart emotionally so their marriage would be as much a sham as his first.

Tearing off her clothes, she stood under the jets of water, hoping she would calm down enough to act rationally.

Afterwards, she unlocked the door and hid her case and travelling bag behind it when it was ajar. Laurel peeked out into the hall to make sure Mac wasn't in sight. Taking a deep breath for courage, she walked to the kitchen.

'Hello, Mrs Evans,' she remarked gaily.

The cook turned her head from

where she was working at the hob and smiled.

'Is Mac around?'

'No, you've just missed him. He left a few minutes ago for the airfield. Do you want some coffee, Laurel? You look as if you could do with some,' Mrs Evans remarked, getting down a mug from the side.

'Please,' she answered, sitting at the large table.

'Have you eaten?' Mrs Evans enquired with an expression of concern as she delivered the steaming mug to her.

'We had a bit for breakfast but I'm not hungry.'

'Nonsense. I'll get you a plate of toast and that'll see you through to lunch time.'

Unable to fight the woman, as she was weak from her outburst, Laurel accepted the large plate of toast with grace but only nibbled several slices before pushing the rest aside.

Mrs Evans pulled out the opposite

chair and sat down.

'You seem troubled, Laurel. Can I help in any way?'

'It's kind of you but I have to sort it out myself,' she replied in a sigh. 'I need some time alone.'

'Sometimes it's best.'

Laurel glanced up from staring at the mahogany.

'Is Jim around? I'd like to ask him if I can use the phone.'

'He's over at the stables, though I'm sure he won't mind seeing as you're a house guest. You can use this one,' Mrs Evans added, pointing to the wall phone. 'I've got to pop out so you'll have privacy.'

'Thank you,' Laurel replied, picking up her handbag and finding her airline ticket wallet.

Waiting until Mrs Evans left, she dialled the contact number in Denver and made a reservation for a connecting flight to New York for that night's departure for Heathrow. She didn't have long as she had to leave the ranch soon to drive to the city's airport.

As an afterthought, she got through to the operator and asked for the dialling code for the United Kingdom. She tapped impatiently while she waited for the phone to be answered.

'Mr Saunders, please,' she informed his secretary. 'This is Laurel Smith and I'm calling from America. Please tell him it's urgent.'

In seconds, he was on the line.

'Laurel? What's happened?'

'I'll explain soon — I'm in a rush. I'm coming home tonight and I don't want you being worried if you see lights on in my house tomorrow.'

'I dropped by yesterday and everything is fine. I've been putting your post in the kitchen.'

'Thanks a lot. I'll come to your office tomorrow.'

'Have you finished?' Mrs Evans suddenly enquired behind her, making Laurel jump guiltily.

'Yes.'

'Jim is coming over now.'

Mrs Evans seemed surprised when Laurel gave her a hug.

'You'll be here for lunch?' she asked Laurel's departing back but she didn't get a reply.

Laurel was taking her bags outside when she met Jim.

'Where are you going, Laurel?'

She set the bags on the wooden porch and threw her arms around him.

'It's too difficult to explain but I promise I'll be in touch.'

'Does Mac know you're leaving?'

'This is very hard for me, Jim. I've grown to love you both but I can't stay. I hope he'll forgive me one day,' she cried up into his kind face. 'Believe me, this is for the best.'

With a final hug, she grabbed her bags and rushed over to her car. Throwing them into the boot, she quickly started up her car, not daring to look around to see if her father was watching her go.

Somehow she managed to control her sobs as she drove down the dusty track and went through the gates on to the main road. She stared ahead as she passed the town's airstrip, not wanting to catch sight of Mac's white car which she knew was there somewhere waiting for his return.

'Oh, I'm so sorry,' she pleaded, driving on.

Only when she reached Denver's Stapleton International airport and had checked in for her flights did she let more tears fall. Huddled in a chair, she waited in the departure lounge, her heart breaking knowing Mac was only a few miles from her.

Would this awful pain ever lessen, she wondered, realising precisely the dilemma her mother had been in and the agony she'd suffered with her choice. Now, Laurel had to live with hers.

9

The rain was lashing down in an English summer deluge and Laurel hurried from the bus stop towards her home, two large bags of groceries in her hands.

She hadn't felt like eating since returning yesterday morning but knew she should force herself. Like her heart, she'd also left her appetite behind in Colorado. Things would never be the same again, she knew, wishing she at least had a photograph to remind herself of the image of the man she loved.

Not that she needed it. Mac's handsome face was etched on her mind, occupying her every waking and sleeping moment. She had caught sight of a man today in town who was of the same build: she'd been upset when he'd turned around and she'd found it wasn't Mac.

Laurel kept her head down and hurried onward, only slowing up when she turned into her gate.

'What the . . . ' One bag fell to the ground, the contents spilling out.

Mac was sitting under her porch, huddled in his raincoat. Getting up, he held her stare as he approached and picked up the scattered tins from the path, replacing them in the carrier.

'Can we go inside?'

Stunned, and feeling extremely guilty, she nodded and brought out her key from her coat pocket. Taking the bag from his hand, she took them out to her kitchen and filled the kettle while she was in there.

'Can I take your coat?' she enquired. The beige mackintosh he peeled off was drenched, and so was his black hair. On this drab, summer afternoon, his tan appeared even darker against the white of his shirt beneath his grey suit.

She took her time hanging it near the

immersion heater and making a pot of tea.

'I didn't expect you to come here.'

'I guessed that from your expression outside,' Mac said, leaning back on the sofa cushions and crossing one suited leg over the other.

Crouching on the floor, she poured out the tea and put one cup on the coffee table in front of him.

'Can I get you a towel for your hair?'

'No! My hair is just fine! I want you to stay in one place long enough so I can get a straight answer from you, Laurel.'

'How did you find me?' she asked, sitting back on her heels.

'With some difficulty as you failed to leave a goodbye note giving us your forwarding address. Why didn't you wait until I got back from Denver and tell me to my face?'

'I couldn't, Mac.' She shrugged. 'I'm a coward.'

'I've come this far to see you so you could at least give me an explanation.'

184

'I've just told you,' she insisted.

'So you feel nothing for me, Laurel, is that it?'

Laurel held her tired head in her hands. She hadn't slept much since that night in the cabin. If only she had the energy to fight him. She mumbled incoherently.

'What did you say, Laurel?'

'I'm suffering badly from jet lag and I don't want to argue.'

'Honey, I've been at my wits' end worrying about what happened to you. It was only when Mrs Evans said you'd spoken on the phone that I contacted the company and they faxed me a detailed report of the outgoing calls. The airline refused to give out any information on your destination, but the other number you dialled was more forthcoming.'

'Mr Saunders.' She groaned.

'I called him from Heathrow when I landed this morning. I told him I had to get hold of you as you'd left something of importance in Colorado.

185

He wouldn't give out your address so we met two hours ago in his office. Why don't you tell me the reason you won't marry me, Laurel?'

She looked up from her hands to find his facial expression stern. He knew why: he knew about Jim. The look on his face said it all.

'I can't, Mac. It's best to leave it as it is rather than get into an argument.'

'I want to hear you say it!' he thundered, his blue eyes blazing.

Tears began to trickle down her pale cheeks and she bit her bottom lip to stop it trembling.

'I have a secret and when you find out, you're going to hate me, Mac,' she cried.

'Try me!' he spat out.

'Only after my mother died, I found out that my natural father was still alive.' Her bloodshot green eyes confronted him. 'Jim Richardson is my dad.'

'I see.'

'It's not what you think.' She got up

and brought back her handbag from the kitchen. Finding her mother's letter, she passed it to Mac. 'Please, read it.'

While he studied it, she returned the snapshot of her parents to its rightful place on the mantelpiece.

'Why did you come looking for him?' he enquired two minutes later.

'Purely out of curiosity,' she replied, not turning to confront him but stroking the silver frame lovingly. 'For years my mum said he was dead and I'd have given anything to have been able to meet him. When I learned he was alive, I rushed over. It was a coincidence we met on the first night I was in town.'

Mac didn't seem to be furious, so she turned around.

'I couldn't believe it when he walked into the restaurant. You can't imagine what it felt like! I meant to keep at a distance but he invited me for a drink when he saw I was alone. I couldn't turn down his invitation to stay at the ranch. I had to get to know my father.'

'And to know what he's worth?'

'How dare you! I knew that's what you'd think, which is why I didn't bring up the subject. I don't care about his money. If I did, I'd have stayed and married you but I'd have been no better than your ex-wife.' Tears flowed now.

'I had to turn my back on my father and the man I love. How easy do you think that was, Mac?' she cried in a rush.

In a split second, Mac was on his feet and his arms were around her.

'Oh, Laurel, we could have sorted it out,' he breathed, hugging her.

'I knew you'd be angry.'

'Have you told Jim?'

She shook her head.

'It didn't seem right. He still loves the memory of my mother and I couldn't hurt him, not even if he was fully fit.'

'I can see now why you were so upset when he had that turn.'

'Having only just found him, I couldn't believe it when he had that attack. I was so distraught.'

Mac kissed the top of her head.

'He was mighty worried, too, when you left suddenly. We had a long talk and he convinced me I should come here.'

'Didn't you want to?' she asked, looking into his face.

'I felt I should leave it a week so you had time to consider everything and get over your journey. When his green eyes pleaded with mine to change my mind, I was suddenly struck by the resemblance. Although Mr Saunders told me you'd gone looking for your father, I already had a pretty good idea why you'd fled.'

As his lips came down on hers, she relished the wonderful sensation that was taking over her body.

'So, Laurel, are you ready to give me your answer?' he asked, pulling back slightly from her mouth.

'Yes — it's yes, Mac.'

Her tears of happiness wet his face as they kissed and laughed and made up for the days they'd been apart.

'So what was it I left behind?' she enquired some time later.

Mac pulled out a small box from his jacket pocket and opened it. On the cream satin lay a diamond ring.

'I can get it adjusted if it's too large,' he told her as he slid it on to her finger and over her knuckle into place.

'It's lovely and it fits perfectly.'

'Though we may have the shortest engagement on record, Laurel. I want us to be married as soon as we can arrange it. Please, come back with me so we can get things moving straight away.'

She smiled up at him, knowing Mr Saunders would be happy to sort out everything in England for her.

'When are we leaving?'

★   ★   ★

Jim was waiting for them in his usual chair on the veranda and Laurel hurried from the car to greet him.

'I'm so glad Mac was able to persuade you to return,' he said, getting up. Laurel threw her arms around him in a tight hug. 'You must be tired after your journey. When Mac phoned from England, I had your room readied so you can rest.'

'Jim, we have to talk,' she said firmly, indicating to the chairs.

She and Mac had discussed the issue at length during the flight and both felt Jim had the right to know the truth. As she sat down, she noticed Mac was deliberately taking his time getting her bags from the car.

Taking a deep breath for courage, she got her mother's letter from her handbag.

'Mac and I are getting married. I would like you to give me away.'

'I'd be delighted, Laurel,' he replied, his green eyes echoing his smile.

'There's something you should read. I've put it off until now because I wasn't sure how you'd take it.' She passed him the letter and regarded his face while he studied it. The creak on the boards as Mac arrived made her glance around.

'I see,' Jim eventually murmured, surprise etched on his features.

'I wanted to tell you,' she urged. 'Really I did.'

Reaching over he took Laurel's trembling hand in his then he stared up at Mac, who was standing by her chair.

'I believe it's customary to ask the father for his daughter's hand in marriage? You already know my prospects are good, Jim.' Mac grinned.

'But I'm a stickler for tradition, son,' he replied, his fingers squeezing Laurel's tightly. 'I never thought I'd ever see this day.' Getting up, he hugged Mac briefly then, turning, took Laurel in his arms.

'Tonight we're gonna have the biggest celebration this place has seen! I just wish Angie was here to see it.'

'She did what she thought was right, Jim,' she said, gazing up at him. 'Is it OK if I call you Dad now?'

192

'Just so long as you let me pay for the wedding.'

She listened while they spoke of the local church where Mac's family had married and of the people they should invite, glad that Jim knew the truth now.

'I should make a contribution as well,' Mac interceded.

'The honeymoon is down to the bridegroom and that's all,' Jim informed him.

'Well, my darling,' Mac said, taking Laurel's hand and kissing it. 'Where would you like to go? We can go anywhere in the world.'

'Anywhere?' she parried with a smile.

He nodded.

'There is one place . . . '

★   ★   ★

Barely four weeks later, Laurel let Mac come around to her door of the Jeep and open it for her. Taking her hand, he helped her down to her feet and the flowing white satin swished across the dust.

'You're a strange woman!' he jested, beaming at her.

'That's a new adjective, Mac. We've only been married four hours and I'm no longer compassionate, loving — '

His kiss stopped her list midway and she put her arms around his neck to extend their caress. He sighed deeply and stepped back from her.

'Though I'm glad you suggested coming here.'

She glanced around the place and nodded. Passion. It was here he'd proclaimed his love for her and it was apt they should spend their first night as husband and wife alone in the deserted town. Strolling arm-in-arm with her new husband, having to go slowly in her full bridal gown she'd insisted on keeping on for the drive, she had never been happier.

'Dad was wonderful today,' she mused, remembering the way he'd proudly walked his daughter up the aisle to Mac and later given a speech at their reception. He said he felt sad that he and Angie hadn't been able to make up their differences then made a toast to absent loved ones which brought a lump to Laurel's throat.

'Your parents must think it's a bit odd that we've come here,' she said, stopping by the house which would be their home for the next week.

'I don't give a hoot what they think, just so long as we're together, Mrs McGuire!'

Laurel chuckled in glee when he suddenly lifted her up and carried her over the open door's threshold.

'What's been going on in here?' she asked as he still held her. There was champagne on ice as well as other food set out. The sofa had been replaced by a new bed and there were two comfortable chairs near the fire.

'I want my gorgeous wife to have the very best,' he drawled, bringing her head down to meet his lips.

Slowly letting her to the ground, their

kiss grew in intensity and Laurel knew that this was the only place they could have come to. Later she would ask him if they could rename the town, because it was becoming more fitting with each passing second, to McGuire's Passion.

THE END

Other titles in the
Linford Romance Library:

VISIONS OF THE HEART

Christine Briscomb

When property developer Connor Grant contracted Natalie Jensen to landscape the grounds of his large country house near Ashley in South Australia, she was ecstatic. But then she discovered he was acquiring — and ripping apart — great swathes of the town. Her own mother's house and the hall where the drama group met were two of his targets. Natalie was desperate to stop Connor's plans — but she also had to fight the powerful attraction flowing between them.

THE PERFECT GENTLEMAN

Liz Pedersen

When Laura agrees to help Anthony Christopher to deceive his family she has no idea how far the web of intrigue will extend, or how it will alter her life. His family is as unpleasant as he promised, but Laura drives away from his funeral thinking she has escaped their malicious clutches. However, this is not so. James Christopher is determined to discover what was behind his cousin's precipitate marriage. He despises Laura and hates the fact that he is attracted to her.

YESTERDAY'S LOVE

Stella Ross

Jessica's return from Africa to claim her inheritance of 'Simon's Cottage', and take up medicine in her home town, is the signal for her past to catch up with her. She had thought the short affair she'd had with her cousin Kirk twelve years ago a long-forgotten incident. But Kirk's unexpected return to England, on a last-hope mission to save his dying son, sparks off nostalgia. It leads Jessica to rethink her life and where it is leading.

THE DOCTOR WAS A DOLL

Claire Vernon

Jackie runs a riding-school and, living happily with her father, feels no desire to get married. When Dr. Simon Hanson comes to the town, Jackie's friends try to matchmake, but he, like Jackie, wishes to remain single and they become good friends. When Jackie's father decides to remarry, she feels she is left all alone, not knowing the happiness that is waiting around the corner.

TO BE WITH YOU

Audrey Weigh

Heather, the proud owner of a small bus line, loves the countryside in her corner of Tasmania. Her life begins to change when two new men move into the area. Colin's charm overcomes her first resistance, while Grant also proves a warmer person than expected. But Colin is jealous when Grant gains special attention. The final test comes with the prospect of living in Hobart. Could Heather bear to leave her home and her business to be with the man she loves?